The Notorious Wolfes

*A powerful dynasty, where secrets and
sc...........................*

Eight siblings, bl.......................... the
one thing ....
A family destroy.................................ver.

THE SECRETS
Haunted by their past and driven to succeed, the
Wolfes scattered to the far corners of the globe.
But secrets never sleep and scandal
is starting to stir….

THE POWER
Now, the Wolfe brothers are back, stronger than
ever, but hiding hearts as hard as granite.
It's said that even the blackest of souls can be
healed by the purest of love…
But can the dynasty rise again?

**Each month, Harlequin Presents® is delighted to
bring you an exciting new installment from
The Notorious Wolfes. You won't want to miss out!**

8 volumes to collect and treasure!

The man's arms were resting nonchalantly on the side of the pool, and crossed, as if he was quite used to hysterical women in full bridal regalia bursting onto his private terrace.

"Shouldn't you be kissing your groom about now?"

His laconically spoken words and their accompanying picture sent a wave of nausea through Aneesa. She had to leave, get away from here. But just as she started to move she realized that her legs had turned to jelly. To her utter horror and chagrin, she folded to the ground from the waist down like a rag doll, the previous minutes' events crippling her.

So quickly that her head spun even more, the man had hauled himself out of the pool and was crouched beside Aneesa, water sluicing off his taut body. Big hands came under her arms and suddenly he was lifting her up as if she weighed no more than a doll.

However handsome she'd thought him before, up close he was quite simply breathtaking. Even though he was a complete stranger Aneesa had the almost overwhelming urge to run her finger along his lower lip and see if his icy blue eyes would darken with the promise of sensual satisfaction.

Abby Green

THE STOLEN BRIDE

TORONTO NEW YORK LONDON
AMSTERDAM PARIS SYDNEY HAMBURG
STOCKHOLM ATHENS TOKYO MILAN MADRID
PRAGUE WARSAW BUDAPEST AUCKLAND

Recycling programs
for this product may
not exist in your area.

ISBN-13: 978-0-373-13012-2

THE STOLEN BRIDE

First published in the UK as *The Restless Billionaire*

First North American Publication 2011

Copyright © 2011 by Harlequin Books S.A.

Special thanks and acknowledgment are given to Abby Green for her
contribution to The Notorious Wolfes series.

All about the author...
Abby Green

ABBY GREEN deferred doing a social anthropology degree to work freelance as an assistant director in the film and TV industry—which is a social study in itself! Since then it's been early starts, long hours, mucky fields, ugly car parks and wet-weather gear—especially working in Ireland. She has no bona fide qualifications but could probably help negotiate a peace agreement between two warring countries after years of dealing with recalcitrant actors. Since discovering a guide to writing romance one day, she decided to capitalize on her longtime love for Harlequin® romances and attempt to follow in the footsteps of such authors as Kate Walker and Penny Jordan. She's enjoying the excuse to be paid to sit inside, away from the elements. She lives in Dublin and hopes that you will enjoy her stories. You can email her at abbygreen3@yahoo.co.uk.

This is for my fellow *The Notorious Wolfes* contributors—Sarah, Janette, Caitlin, Lynn, Robyn, Jennie and Kate, thanks for all your help and encouragement along the way!

CHAPTER ONE

ANEESA ADANI was stuck in a waking nightmare. She battled a surge of panic as her younger sister and aunts led her forward towards the place where her fiancé waited to make her his wife.

The elaborate wedding sari she wore constricted her movements, adding to the sense of cloying claustrophobia. Heavy jewels literally dripped from her head, ears, throat, arms and hands, weighing her down.

Fighting an overwhelming urge to break free and escape she told herself once again that she only had herself to blame for her predicament. If she hadn't been so blinkered, so unforgivably naïve...so impossibly complacent, then she might not be here right now.

She was propelled forward again and suddenly her fiancé and her parents saw her arrival. A hush descended over the crowd in the huge and beautiful inner courtyard, lit with the seductive glow of hundreds of lanterns. This courtyard was the centrepiece in one of the most exclusive hotels in Mumbai—the jewel in the hotel's crown. The sheer opulence of it all terrified her now, the reality of what she was doing hitting her anew.

With an awful sick feeling of impending doom and

fatality Aneesa reluctantly moved forward, but just then a small movement caught her eye from the side. She glanced around and, for a moment, was blinded by the icy blue gaze of a man. He was slightly obscured, in the shadows, but even that couldn't hide the fact that he was so tall and good-looking he momentarily distracted her from her surroundings.

As she registered the darkly handsome foreigner who had no doubt snuck in to ogle the most prestigious wedding of the year, reality slammed back into her again, heightened now by seeing him—as if he represented some kind of escape or freedom to her. And she knew in that moment that she hadn't been able to disguise the fear or turmoil in her eyes. He'd seen it all and she could only be thankful that he was a complete stranger. Tearing her eyes away, she mentally steeled herself and walked forward to meet her fate....

Sebastian Wolfe still reeled slightly from the searing glance he'd shared with the bride as she'd arrived. She'd looked around only briefly and yet had honed in on his gaze as if she'd felt the weight of it.

He shrugged off the prickling sensation. He had to admit that he didn't think he'd ever seen a more beautiful bride. He smiled cynically—not that he ever had any intention of watching one walk down an aisle towards *him*. Coming from a large family of mainly half-siblings, having been born to a man who'd married three times, had numerous affairs and begat eight children, to say that Sebastian had a jaundiced view of the holy sanctity of marriage was a huge understatement.

With an iron will, he concentrated once more on his surroundings and not the potential minefield of his family, who had dispersed from their ancestral home, Wolfe Manor, as soon as they'd been able to escape.

In the huge and ornately decorated inner courtyard a stunning marquee covered in silken swathes of material took up the centre space under a dusky evening sky. The bride, while being of average height, stood with a regal and graceful bearing that made her appear taller.

Her face was a smooth mask of intent concentration, and given the elaborate ritual of the traditional Indian wedding, he couldn't blame her. It seemed to him to consist of a dizzying array of minutely observed events, each as important as the last and all following a strict code. It had been going on for days now, culminating in this ceremony here tonight. Incense was burning, ladening the warm air around him with a rich and luxuriant smell.

A short while before, Sebastian had watched the arrival of the groom carried aloft on a gold chair, where, bedecked in a long tunic of spun silken gold and close-fitting matching trousers, he'd been greeted by his in-laws, his face obscured by a curtain of fresh marigold flowers.

And then the bride had been brought in, her slender arms encased in silver, red and gold bangles, led by attendant women. Sebastian had seen the intricate henna tattoo that adorned her hands up as far as her lower arms. In her glittering red-and-gold sari and elaborate headdress and with a pearl-and-diamond jewel nestling at the centre of her forehead, she'd looked like an Indian princess from the Mogul Empire.

The memory of the look they'd shared hit him again with a jolt of sensation in his solar plexus. It was bizarre, but he thought he'd seen something close to panic and desperation in her huge brown, heavily kohled eyes.

He frowned; he must have been mistaken, because now, as he watched the bride and groom place garlands over each other's heads, she looked nothing but serene. And yet, had he just seen her delicate hands shaking? Sebastian mentally chastised himself—what did he care for the emotional state of a complete stranger on her wedding day? All he cared about was that everything went smoothly and they had no cause to fault their venue.

This hotel was just one in his hugely successful chain of hotels around the world. The uberluxurious Mumbai Grand Wolfe Hotel. And he was here merely on a whirlwind tour to oversee the society wedding of the year: Aneesa Adani to Jamal Kapoor Khan, two of Bollywood's hottest stars.

From the report his Indian PA had given him about the wedding, he knew that Aneesa Adani had been crowned Miss India some years before and following a successful modelling career she'd branched into Bollywood movies and had since become their biggest star, with a veritable list of number-one movies to her credit. The subsequent romance and wedding with fellow Bollywood star Jamal Kapoor Khan was going to make them the power couple of Indian cinema for years to come. They were at the very epicentre of mass adulation, which in a country of more than a billion people was no small feat.

Sebastian cast a quick look around, noting to his satisfaction the heavily armed security guards and plainclothed police officers, amongst his own highly trained security team. Nothing had been left to chance and he was quietly confident of the strict security measures and discretion he could guarantee in all of his hotels. It was one of the reasons his hotel had been picked as the venue of choice for this wedding as well as for its ultralavish yet understated stylish surroundings.

From where he stood he could see the rising moon shining over the Arabian Sea and the floodlit outline of the Gateway of India, Mumbai's most iconic landmark.

Sebastian waited for the usual sense of satisfaction to steal over him when he experienced a moment like this—the rare chance to stand back and survey his hard work. A moment when he lifted his head long enough to acknowledge the fruits of his success. But it didn't come. And it was only then that he realised that he hadn't felt it in some time.

Unused to and slightly disturbed by that thought and the impulse to self-examine which he didn't usually indulge in, he looked once again to the centre of the marquee where the bride and groom now sat side by side on regal thrones on a raised dais.

The bride's exquisite face was still a cool mask of serenity but Sebastian felt the hairs rise on the back of his neck as if he could somehow sense that it was just a façade.

And then he felt a pull of something much more earthy in his groin. Encased in the elaborate wedding costume he could only see snatches of her pale olive skin, an enticing view of the bare curve of her waist and top of her hip below the tight bodice. He could imagine the silky texture of that skin, that it would feel as soft as a fresh rose petal.

To his utter chagrin and disgust, Sebastian realised

that he was ogling a *bride* in the midst of her wedding ceremony and that merely looking at her was arousing him to a level that he hadn't felt since his last liaison had ended some weeks previously. He realised, too, that on some very base level he felt *jealous* of the groom, that he would be the one to uncover the lush secrets of his new wife's exotic beauty.

Sebastian cursed himself. He'd no doubt that Aneesa Adani was like every other girl of her upper-middle-class upbringing. A little princess. Her marriage to this man was merely the next step in a life of luxury and inherent idleness, despite her career as an actress. And he'd no doubt, too, that she would be no blushing virgin on her wedding night. Despite the chaste lovemaking of the Bollywood movies, in the real world the stars were just as amoral and prone to bed-hopping as in Hollywood, and she'd had a highly publicised relationship with this man for months.

Despite those assertions, turning away took more effort than he liked to acknowledge and he saw one of his close aides waiting patiently in the wings for his next move. Sebastian welcomed the distraction and thrust aside disturbing thoughts of flashing kohled eyes that had emitted what must have been an imaginary beacon of distress, and equally disturbing erotic images of sensual half-hidden curves.

He walked out of the courtyard, leaving the wedding behind, and smiled grimly. His mind had been playing tricks on him, perhaps the ritual and incense had gotten to him for a moment. Striding across the main reception area which was a glorious fusion of classic Moorish and Portuguese design, he coolly ignored the admiring looks his tall and powerful frame drew. The attention of women was something that Sebastian and his brothers had never had to worry about. They'd effortlessly drawn it as soon as they'd been old enough to know what that attention meant.

Minutes later, after consulting with his hotel manager, he stepped into his private lift and felt the habitual constriction of being in a suit, and the familiar need to engage in something physical which would clear and quieten his mind. Exercise for Sebastian was a drug, an outlet he'd turned to for as long as he could remember. It had helped him escape the chaos of his dysfunctional upbringing and now helped him escape the rigid confines on his time. It also eased the niggling sense of dissatisfaction he increasingly felt, and helped him through the frequent nights where he was lucky to get three hours sleep, the curse of the chronic insomniac.

Sebastian didn't register the impassive lines of his hard-boned face in the mirrored elevator door; he'd long ago learnt the art of projecting a controlled front, even while inwardly he might be a mass of contradictions. But his thoughts helplessly veered back to the couple downstairs. He had no doubt that in time reality would strike and the sham that all marriages inevitably were would become apparent in theirs. And in a country which held one of the lowest divorce rates in the world he could almost feel a twinge of sympathy for the happy couple, for it was unlikely they'd be allowed to escape the confines of their union, especially if they had children.

He chastised himself mockingly—who was he to rain on their parade or judge them? His mouth tightened with grim black humour—after all, hadn't he himself come from a far from normal family upbringing?

On that thought the elevator doors opened and
Sebastian walked into the penthouse Grand Wolfe
suite, the best in the hotel. As he started to rip off his
tie and jacket he mentally wished the couple downstairs
all the best in the world and firmly pushed the image of
the luscious bride from his mind. They were welcome
to each other and a lifetime of wedded disharmony.

Aneesa was barely aware of the wedding ritual going
on around her. She felt numb from the inside out and
she knew on some level that this feeling was a form of
self-protection, albeit dangerously flimsy.

Her head ached as it had done ever since her comfortable, privileged and secure world had been blown to
smithereens just two evenings previously. She'd gone to
Jamal's rooms at the hotel to surprise him, hoping that
she might encourage him to take their chaste lovemaking to the next level.

The thought of being a virgin on her wedding night
had inexplicably filled Aneesa with fear; perhaps even
then she'd been aware that what she and Jamal shared
wasn't normal and had wanted to provoke him in some
way. She'd never understood his reticence in the physical side of their relationship.

But instead of finding him quietly reading his
new script, which is what he'd told her he'd be doing,
she'd found him in bed. With his assistant. His *male*
assistant.

Aneesa knew she still hadn't fully assimilated the
shock of that moment. She'd stumbled to the bathroom
and had been violently ill. By then Jamal's lover had
disappeared and Jamal had calmed down enough to go
into damage limitation mode.

She could remember his smoothly handsome face, a mask of condescending pity, as he'd asked her how she hadn't already known about this when all their friends knew. And Aneesa had almost been sick again when she'd recalled the snide looks she'd often dismissed as petty jealousy from their circle of friends. She'd also had to acknowledge uncomfortably that of her so-called friends who even now thronged the courtyard of this exclusive hotel, there hadn't been one she'd felt she could confide in.

It had been a harsh pill to swallow to acknowledge how shallow her life had become, and how easily she'd left good friends behind once she'd become more and more famous.

In the space of that one evening, her whole life had undergone a subtle but seismic shift. And in the couple of days since, Aneesa had changed from being a relatively spoilt young woman, who'd pretty much taken everything around her for granted, into someone more mature and less naïve. The urge to find comfort in blame had been futile, for she knew she was as much to blame for the situation she now found herself in, as painful as it was to acknowledge that.

Jamal's curt warning from that evening still rang in her ears and it had fatally inhibited her impulse to ask for help or advice: 'If you think for a second that you can walk away from this marriage you can kiss your career goodbye for ever. Who would want to marry you after such a scandal? Because you can be sure of one thing, if you walk away and try to save face by telling people the truth, I will deny it and fight you every step of the way. This marriage is my ticket to respectability for ever. Our children will make everyone believe that we have the perfect marriage. And who would even believe you over me? Their beloved Jamal Kapoor Khan?'

Aneesa had known he was right. If she even attempted to reveal the truth she'd be crucified by his millions of devoted fans. As famous as she was, he was a far bigger star. She'd be a pariah and would never make another movie in India. Apart from all of that, she was the first in her family to get married. Her beloved paternal grandmother was nearing ninety and maintaining that she was clinging onto dear life just long enough to see Aneesa wed.

Aneesa also knew that while the public perception of her family was that they had untold wealth, in fact, her father had been struggling to keep the family silk business afloat for some time now. Only she and her mother knew the reality, which was that this wedding was all but crippling her father financially.

And yet, Aneesa also knew that her father would prefer to face financial ruin than the ignomy of not being able to pay for his first daughter's marriage. He was so proud that he hadn't even let Aneesa help financially. While her pay packet was nothing like her Hollywood counterparts, by Indian standards she was a wealthy woman in her own right.

And how could she have told her parents about Jamal's secret? They were conservative and solidly middle class. Respectability was their middle name; they would be devastated. The pressure in her head and behind her eyes suddenly increased now in an intense physical pain.

She could feel the weight of Jamal's gaze from her left and could barely bring herself to turn to him, anticipating all too well the false adoration that would be written all over his handsome features. It was a look that he'd perfected over many years in films. A look that she'd fallen for herself when they'd met on her first film, and a look that she'd fooled herself into believing was sincere.

No wonder he'd wooed her so easily, she recognised now with acrid bitterness. He'd seen her coming from a mile away: sheltered, spoilt, immature and unbelievably naïve. And she'd fallen for his act, hook, line and sinker—seduced by his smooth good looks and even smoother talking. Not to mention his intense attention and adulation of her. He'd appealed to all the worst parts of her and she'd live with the shame of that for the rest of her life.

Her train of thought and self-disgust was cut short abruptly when the priest officiating indicated for them to stand. They were approaching the most sacred part of the ceremony, after which Aneesa knew her chances of escape would be all but gone for ever.

The ends of her sari and Jamal's long jacket were tied together and they were about to walk around the sacred fire seven times, while seven blessings were said, each one for different aspects of their marriage. As they started to walk slowly around the fire, Aneesa felt again the rising tide of panic. The numbness was leaving her now and in its place she began to shake and tremble in reaction to what she was doing.

Any girlish dreams she'd had of falling in love and marrying had long since been turned to dust. Her eyes were wide open now and with each step she took with Jamal around this fire, she was hurtling further into a future with no escape and certain pain and suffering.

How could she possibly bring children into a marriage like that? When their father would be sleeping with their mother purely to procreate and maintain a façade?

In that second Aneesa recalled the piercing blue eyes of the man she'd seen in the shadows and suddenly an impulse stronger than anything she'd ever felt rushed through her. In the midst of the shock and panic she acted with an economy and sureness of movement that surprised her. She stopped and bent and swiftly undid the knot that tied her sari to Jamal's coat. She barely heard his indrawn breath and his hissed, 'Aneesa… what do you think you are doing?'

Then she stepped off the dais. Heart thumping she went straight to her open-mouthed father and took his hand in hers. She was aware that everyone was frozen in shock and surprise and knew dimly that she had to take advantage of that. She brought her father's hand to her mouth and pressed a kiss against it and said with a hoarse voice, her eyes filling with tears, 'I'm so sorry, Papa, I can't do this. I'll pay you back. Please forgive me.'

And she fled.

Aneesa was barely aware of where she'd run, she knew only that she wouldn't have long to capitalise on the shock of the wedding crowd before her father sent people to find her. She couldn't bear to think of her parents' confusion and dismay either, or else she'd falter altogether. And she couldn't turn back now.

She stopped for a moment, her heart hammering in her chest. She'd come up several flights of service stairs and now saw what looked like a staff elevator. All

Aneesa hoped for was that it would take her somewhere far away from that courtyard and somewhere quiet, where she could assess the situation she now found herself in. She longed for fresh air, and her clothes felt more constrictive than ever.

The elevator slid silently upwards, and then came to a smooth halt. The doors opened with a muted whoosh and she found herself in what looked like a utility room. Albeit a very plush utility room.

She approached the one door and opened it with her heart in her mouth. Peering out she could see that she was in a suite of rooms that went on and on. All was quiet and still. No one was here. She automatically assumed that she'd found one of the empty suites in this massive hotel. Heaving a huge sigh of relief, she emerged more fully and walked into a darkened kitchen. She could see a huge formal dining room and, through that, wall-to-wall sliding glass doors which led to an open terrace and balcony outside. She could see the skyline of Mumbai laid out like a glittering carpet. This was no ordinary suite, this was the penthouse!

When she thought of her own honeymoon suite with its king-size bed covered in rose petals she felt clammy and sweaty all over again. Almost tripping in her long sari she made for the glass doors, struggling to open them and get out to the fresh air.

Finally they slid back and Aneesa stumbled out, gasping now. She ripped the heavy garland of flowers from around her neck and let it fall to the ground. She was vaguely aware of a dim light coming from nearby but barely registered it. When she reached the wall she tipped her head back and breathed deep, the chaotic sounds of the crazy Mumbai traffic drifting up from far, far below.

Her heart finally started to slow down. So when she heard a deep drawling voice say, 'Please don't tell me you're thinking of jumping…' Aneesa screamed.

CHAPTER TWO

ANEESA whirled around so fast her head spun and she gripped the wall behind her with both hands. And then she saw him in the dim light. She recognised him instantly by his intense piercing blue eyes, like chips of ice. It was the man from the shadows she'd seen downstairs. And now she also registered what she'd missed entirely in her distraught state: a state-of-the-art terrace pool, lit from underwater.

The man's arms were resting nonchalantly on the side of the pool, and crossed, as if he was quite used to hysterical women in full bridal regalia bursting onto his private terrace.

His hair was slicked back against a well-shaped skull and in the shadows the lines of his face were stark, his jaw hard. He arched one ebony-black brow and once again Aneesa had the gut-clenching realisation of how extraordinarily handsome he was. It was a physical sensation she'd never experienced with Jamal, even though she'd believed herself to be in love with him. The realisation sent shock through her system.

'Shouldn't you be kissing your groom about now?'

His laconically spoken words and their accompanying picture sent a wave of nausea through Aneesa.

Barely thinking, she said numbly, 'All Jamal will be concerned about is his precious reputation.'

Hearing her own voice loud in the silence made shock grip her anew. She had to leave. Get away from here, but just as she started to move she realised that her legs had turned to jelly. To her utter horror and chagrin, she folded to the ground from the waist down like a rag doll, the previous minutes' events crippling her.

So quickly, that she didn't have time to register, the man had hauled himself out of the pool and was crouched beside Aneesa, water sluicing off his taut body. Big hands came under her arms and suddenly he was lifting her up as if she weighed no more than a doll.

Amidst the shock of reality hitting her, and his proximity, a torrent of words clamoured to get out. 'I'm so… sorry…had no idea anyone was here. I ran…had to get away. I'll go…leave you alone…shouldn't be here…'

Aneesa was aware that her teeth were chattering and that the man was effortlessly supporting her as he led her back through the doors and into a luxurious living room, switching on low lights as he went. His arm around her was like a steel support, and the wet body she could feel through her sari felt like a warm wall of hard muscle.

He brought her over to a sumptuous couch and sat her down with a gentleness that belied his obvious strength. When she was seated he crouched down and looked up into her face. However handsome she'd thought him before, up close he was quite simply breathtaking.

Even though his hair was wet, she could see that it was cut almost militarily short. His blue eyes were deep set, over a patrician nose which gave him a look of royalty. A thin upper lip spoke of a cool control, but his full lower lip spoke of passion and an innate sensuality, and even though he was a complete stranger Aneesa had the almost overwhelming urge to run her finger along that lower lip and see if his icy blue eyes would darken with the promise of sensual satisfaction.

Aghast at the totally uncharacteristic and wanton direction of her thoughts she recoiled back and then wished she hadn't as it gave her a better view of his broad shoulders and tautly muscled chest, covered with a smattering of masculine hair.

Something flashed in his eyes and he drew back too, asking, 'Will you be OK for a minute if I go and put some clothes on?'

Aneesa's head nearly fell off she nodded it so vigorously. She couldn't even speak and just watched with a dry mouth as he stood to his full imposing height, and strode away. Helplessly, her eyes drawn to the sheer athletic grace with which he walked. He had a broad back, which tapered down to narrow hips and then lower to where his short swim trunks hugged the globes of his muscular bottom. His skin was a burnished olive as if he spent much time outdoors, and dimly she wondered if he might be some sort of professional athlete.

With a flood of heat rising from her belly upwards Aneesa finally dragged her gaze away and groaned, bringing her hands to her face. What was wrong with her? She'd just sent her whole life into a tailspin and here she was drooling over some stranger's half-naked body.

The only thing stopping her from getting up and running at that moment was a curious sense of lethargy and also the very real fear that she'd collapse again. Also she owed this man an explanation for bursting into his penthouse suite. She told herself she'd just wait till he came back and then apologise and leave, and hopefully by then she'd be in a fit enough state to walk out with some measure of dignity, and find some other sanctuary where she could lick her wounds.

Sebastian stepped out from under the cold spray of the quickest shower he'd ever taken and roughly ran a towel over his body. He'd had to take a cold shower because merely putting his hands under Aneesa Adani's arms when he'd helped her inside had unleashed a flood of desire so forceful that he'd nearly lost control.

He could still feel the gentle swell of her breast against his side, the silky brush of her hair as it had swung against him and an enticing scent of exotic flowers. Her skin was as soft as he'd imagined it might be earlier.

He cursed himself as his body started to respond to the mental images again and he enforced rigid control, dragging on a pair of black trousers and a white shirt. Clearly she didn't feel the same level of intensely immediate attraction if the way she'd recoiled just now was anything to go by. And what the *hell* was she doing here anyway? She should be in the midst of her wedding right now, and yet she'd looked like a car crash victim. Albeit the most beautiful car crash victim he'd ever seen.

Grimly he recognised that he obviously hadn't misread her look earlier. Her mouth… He had to grit his jaw just thinking of how it had trembled. How she'd pressed those lips together to try and contain her emotion. And how it had made him want to reach up and pull her head down to his so that he could press his mouth against hers and see if she tasted as sweet as she looked.

He'd just finished his first punishing set of lengths when she'd burst onto the terrace and for a second he'd believed he might be hallucinating. Or going mad. He'd spoken out loud as much to dispel the image before him, but then she'd screamed and turned around, clearly stunned to find anyone there. And as soon as he'd realised that she was very real, his brain had gone into meltdown.

Chagrined to be brought to this level of lack of control, Sebastian took a deep breath and went back out to the living room.

Aneesa heard the stranger returning and stood, but almost immediately she swayed. In a second he was by her side again—and dressed, she noted with relief. He pushed her back down onto the couch gently.

His voice was grim. 'You're not in any state to go anywhere.'

Before Aneesa could protest he was handing her a glass which held about an inch of dark golden liquid. She looked up and said huskily, 'I don't drink.'

He held it out. 'Consider it medicinal. You need something, you're clearly in shock.'

Belatedly she noted the English intonation of his accent. With a slight tremor in her hands she took the glass, relieved that their fingers didn't touch, and wrinkling her nose, she took a sip, wincing as the fiery liquid burnt its way down her throat. Almost immediately she could feel it settle into her stomach and a resulting warm numbing glow spread outwards.

She sensed rather than saw him move away and when she could muster the courage she looked up to see him standing a few feet away with arms crossed, leaning insouciantly against the glass doors. The white of his shirt couldn't disguise the powerful chest underneath, or the way the muscles in his arms bunched. He watched her intently and she flushed.

She bit her lip and then said, 'I'm very sorry for disturbing you like this. I had no right to barge in.'

He frowned then, black brows drawing together over those mesmerising eyes. 'How *did* you get in?'

Aneesa faltered for a moment, much of her journey here was hazy. 'I think through a service lift, into a utility room...'

His mouth tightened with displeasure and Aneesa read it to mean that he was angry with her. She started to apologise again. 'I'm so sorry—really, I had no idea where I was going—'

He cut her off. 'It's not your fault.'

Just then a phone rang, making Aneesa flinch. Her heart started to hammer again and she looked from the phone on a nearby table to the man in horror. 'They must be looking for me....'

As he pushed himself away from the glass doors he said, 'I'll have to answer it or they'll send someone up.'

Aneesa stood in agitation, still gripping the glass. 'Please, don't tell them I'm here. *Please.* I'm not ready to deal with...it.'

She watched as the man picked up the phone, answering with a curt, 'Yes,' his eyes never leaving hers.

Aneesa could just hear an indistinctly panicked voice. They must be phoning every room in the hotel. Her heart sank. This man was a complete stranger; he had no obligation to protect her. But even as she was thinking this and fearing the worst he cut off the babble on the phone and said, 'I've seen no one. Please don't disturb me again tonight unless it's urgent. I'm sure the manager can deal with the situation.'

And he put down the phone. His eyes hadn't left hers for a second.

Relief washed through Aneesa, dizzying in its intensity, even as her skin tingled, as if something unspoken had just passed between them. 'Thank...thank you so much, I know you have no obligation to help me....'

The man prowled close to her and took the glass from her white-knuckled grip, placing it down on a table. Curiously, she recognised that even though she didn't know him, she felt safe with him. As if she could trust him. And that was a revelation when for days she'd looked at everyone around her with suddenly jaundiced eyes.

He straightened up again to his full intimidating height. 'Perhaps we should introduce ourselves, because it looks like you won't be going anywhere for a while. They have every guard combing the hotel for you right now. I think you must be aware that I know who you are.'

Up until recently she would have automatically expected that response, but while this man knew who she was, clearly he wasn't in thrall and that gave Aneesa a heady feeling. New humility and untold gratitude for this sanctuary made her voice soft. 'Yes, I'm Aneesa.'

After a long moment she put out her hand, only

becoming belatedly aware of what a caricature she must look like with the henna tattoo and all the elaborate jewels, and the wedding outfit. Her hand was enveloped in his much larger one, his grip warm and strong and sending a disturbing electric tingle right to her groin. He smiled and it was lopsided, making Aneesa feel dizzy again. She feared after tonight that she'd never get her equilibrium back.

'Sebastian…at your service it would seem.' Sebastian had made a split-second decision not to mention his family name, feeling it hanging like a yoke around his neck, and was aware for the first time that he was in the presence of someone who didn't appear to know who he was. The thought was curiously heady.

A thread of illicit tension snaked through Aneesa at his words. As if he might be at her service in a much more carnal way. Shocked by that thought, and suddenly overwhelmed by everything and feeling more and more ridiculous, she said shakily, 'Would you mind if I used your bathroom?'

He stood back after a long moment, releasing her hand with deliberate slowness, and shook his head, gazing so intently at her that she felt flutters run all the way up and down her spine. No man had ever looked at her so explicitly. He gestured to the back of the penthouse. 'By all means, it's just through there.'

Aneesa walked away on still-wobbly legs and found the bathroom, slipping inside and closing the door. It was a relief to be away from that courtyard and the intense pressure, and a relief to be away from Sebastian's disturbing presence. Just then she remembered how it had been the memory of his eyes that had acted as a catalyst to make her run from the ceremony.

And now she was here, in *his* suite. And he was protecting her from the hordes.

She shivered slightly. She was a pragmatic person, not given to flights of fancy, but it suddenly felt very serendipitous to have arrived here. Immediately that visceral physical response flooded her body in a way that had never happened before.

Even on the fateful evening she'd gone to Jamal's room to seduce him in her impossibly naïve way, she'd felt no physical anticipation, and yet in the space of the past few minutes she'd become more aware of herself and another man than she ever had been in her whole life. It was fast eclipsing the recent disastrous events.

She pushed away from the door and went to stand in front of the mirror; a soft light had come on automatically once she'd opened the door of the bathroom. She sighed deeply. When had she become so used to, or expected, such flippant luxuries?

She looked at her heavily made-up face and urgently wanted to feel clean again. As if she could get rid of the persona of Aneesa Adani, Bollywood's darling. She released the clip which held the jewel that sat in the centre of her forehead and laid it down carefully and with warm water in the sink she bent and splashed it over her face.

After a few minutes though, she could see that it was going to take a lot more than water to wipe it all away. A sense of futility washed through her and also pain, to know the upheaval she was undoubtedly causing within her family. Jamal she wasn't unduly concerned about; he would survive, especially now she knew he'd only seen her as a strategic pawn.

But her parents…they had deserved better. She could

picture the disappointment and humiliation on their faces right now. They loved her so much, and while she knew they were proud of her success, she knew that they'd have been equally proud if she'd become a housewife and had babies. They'd always accepted her unconditionally and this is how she repaid them....

Emotion surged; Aneesa was unable to stop gut-wrenching sobs from rising upwards. She hadn't really lost control yet, and the pressure of keeping it together nearly floored her now. She pulled at the bangles on her arms and rings on her fingers, uncaring of the pain as she ripped them off, dropping them to the counter. With shaking hands she untied the necklace from around her neck and it, too, fell under its own heavy weight.

Sobbing now in earnest, and with a sense of inner desperation mounting and anger at herself once again for having been so stupid and selfish, she tried ineffectually to wash the henna tattoo off her arms and hands, knowing that all the scrubbing in the world wouldn't remove it, only the passing of time.

Just then a knock came on the door, and Sebastian's voice saying, 'Aneesa, are you all right in there?'

She couldn't answer; the tears were streaming down her face now, streaking it with mascara. Her chest heaved with jerky sobs and she sagged back against the sink just as Sebastian opened the door, took one look and strode in.

She held out her dripping hands stupidly and looked up at him, struggling to regain control. 'I...I can't get rid of the henna tattoo.... Do you have any idea what this means?'

Sebastian shook his head, looking grim. And gorgeous. Aneesa was aware of that even in this state.

She said brokenly, 'It's meant to symbolise my transition from innocence…except now I don't even have a husband to seduce me! I'm going to be walking around with the physical mark of my shame for everyone to see for weeks!'

Sebastian just got a facecloth and wrung it out in the warm water. He came close and gently wiped at the trails of mascara running down Aneesa's cheeks. She could feel the backs of his lower arms brush against her chest as he wiped her face, and in an instantaneous reaction, her nipples stiffened, pushing against the hard material of her bodice top. Her inner agitation died away as a wholly new tension entered her body, flooding her belly with a hot tingling awareness, a sensation of melting.

A taut stillness entered the air around them as Sebastian washed her face. He finally put the cloth down and took a towel, drying Aneesa's hands.

Then he dropped the towel and brought his hands to Aneesa's jaw, his thumbs brushing back and forth against her cheeks. She was barely breathing now, hypnotised by the blue glitter of his eyes, by the heady sense of expectation in the air, by his intensely masculine scent. She could see his jaw clench as if he was exerting some control and inwardly a hidden part of her trembled to think that he had to exert it because of *her*.

He didn't step away; he didn't take his hands from her jaw or face, and Aneesa felt like she was slowly being set on fire. Her gaze slipped down to his mouth and she ached to know how it would feel be to be kissed by him. She'd never been properly kissed by any man, thanks to her sheltered upbringing and then the even more sheltered world of being Jamal Kapoor Khan's love interest, on and off the screen.

Sebastian's virile masculinity wound around her like a spell, rendering her oblivious to everything but him and this moment in time. Making her forget everything.

He asked with a gruff voice, 'What did you mean when you said your fiancé would only be concerned about his reputation?'

Aneesa blinked and welcomed his breaking of the seductive spell, but with that came the emotion surging again. Sebastian held her steady even when she felt one or two tears slip out, his thumbs merely catching them.

'I couldn't marry him. It would have been a lie. I could have done it if it was just for myself and to save my family from the shame…but he expected us to have children. And I couldn't bear the thought of bringing a child into such a façade….'

Sebastian frowned. 'What façade? What do you mean?'

Aneesa tried to look down but Sebastian tipped her chin back up, not letting her escape. And in all honesty there was a part of her aching to tell someone about what had happened. And who better than a practical stranger she'd never meet again?

'Jamal is gay. His assistant has been his lover for years. Everyone knew apparently except me….' Bitterness tinged her voice. 'And I didn't know because I was so wrapped up in myself, in believing that everyone loved me and that my life was all perfect. I only found out because I walked in on him and his lover a couple of days ago.

'He wanted to marry to project an image of respectability. Homosexuality might be legal now but it's still taboo here, especially in Bollywood. His career would be over if people found out. And I was the perfect fool for him to seduce....'

Aneesa avoided Sebastian's eyes now, terrified she'd see his disgust and pity. But his hands just tightened on her jaw, tipping it up again so that she couldn't avoid his gaze. There was no pity in his eyes, only an intense *heat*. She felt as if she were being scorched alive from the inside out and there was a curious ache in the pit of her belly, an ache she knew instinctively that only *he* could assuage.

Sebastian was unable to stop a visceral emotion from rising; her eyes were two huge almond-shaped pools of dark brown, long lashed and full of swirling emotions. 'You're so beautiful....'

The old Aneesa would have taken the compliment for granted. But now all she could think of to say was, 'So are you.'

Sebastian let her face go but only to take her hand in his and lead her out of the bathroom.

Once in the living room again Aneesa tugged free of Sebastian's grip. Instantly she felt bereft, but fear of the way this man was making her feel so instantly out of control made her panicky. As if she were on a runaway train going faster and faster. 'I should really go. I can't impose on you anymore.'

She saw something indefinable flash in his eyes but he just said laconically, 'You're ready to go out there and take on the fallout of the bride fleeing the most high-profile wedding of the year? The place will be swarming with press by now.'

Aneesa felt the blood drain from her face to remember what lay outside this suite and heard Sebastian curse softly. He came close again but she stopped him with a hand and then looked down as if momentarily mesmerised. She looked back up and tried to smile wryly. 'Do you know that ever since I was a little girl I dreamt of the day I'd get married? I fantasised about the Mehendi ceremony. All of my cousins and female relations gathered to witness the drawing of the intricate henna design on my hands and feet…in preparation for my husband to discover on our wedding night.'

Her smile wobbled. 'And yet when it came to my wedding, I insisted on a top Bollywood make-up artist and wouldn't let my female relatives have anything to do with it. At the last minute I tried to change it, but the make-up artist kicked up such a fuss that I couldn't.…'

It suddenly hit Aneesa then, the very real probability that she would not have a second chance to have the wedding night of her childhood dreams. No chance to make reparations with her relatives and do it properly.

An awful gaping emptiness wrenched her insides, the loss of a lifelong dream profound, even as she recognised that the wedding she'd just run from had been a million miles from the dream she'd visualised as a child anyway.

She looked at Sebastian and said huskily, 'I'll never have that first night with my husband.' She gestured with a hand over her whole outfit. 'This is all… wasted.'

Sebastian's face was implacable, stern, and Aneesa could sense in that moment that he rarely lost control. And suddenly, Aneesa felt an overwhelming urge to see him lose that control. She had no idea where it was coming from but it was rising and gathering force within her.

Without even realising what she was doing she'd moved closer to Sebastian and she saw his eyes flare, bright blue. It emboldened something deep inside her. She blurted out without thinking, 'I wish I'd met you…I wish that my first night could have been with you.'

Aneesa knew on some dim level the enormity of what she had said, but her heart had slowed to a steady deep beat, her blood was pooling low in her belly and her gaze dropped to Sebastian's mouth. She was simply speaking the truth and couldn't have held it back even if she'd wanted to.

Everything within Sebastian narrowed to this moment. Arousal so fierce that it was almost painful gripped him. Did she know what she was saying? Was she a virgin? That thought should be sending him running, fast, in the opposite direction. But it wasn't; it was having an even more incendiary effect on his blood. Aneesa was looking at his mouth, her lips parting, eyes glowing like dark jewels, and he couldn't resist—he had to taste her, touch her. *Kiss her.*

Abruptly Aneesa tried to back away, the sudden dawning of realisation in her eyes, and her cheeks flushing with what had to be embarrassment. Registering her emotion made Sebastian feel inordinately protective. He reached for her and captured her easily, spanning two hands around her slim waist, bare under the drape of the sari, her skin satin soft.

Gently, yet with unmistakable remorselessness, he pulled her towards him and bent his head. Never before had he been so achingly aware of every small move, the delicious anticipation of kissing a woman for the first time.

Aneesa was powerless to resist Sebastian's attraction. When he'd pulled her closer he had looked as if he wanted to consume her whole, and fire exploded along every vein in her body.

His mouth was so close now... Aneesa could feel her eyes flutter closed, the intensity of feelings within her almost unbearable. And then their breaths mingled, his firm mouth touched hers and she was lost in a heady world of sensation that obliterated all the pain and turmoil as effectively as if she'd just lost her memory.

The kiss started off slow and gentle, a sensual exploration that made her tremble all over. Sebastian's hands moved up from her waist to hold her head loosely, fingers caressing her skull. She could feel her already unravelling hair coming loose.

He coaxed her lips apart and when she felt his tongue explore her open mouth to touch her tongue in an intimate caress, she gasped and fresh heat flooded into her belly, making her press her legs together when a pulse throbbed between them.

In a heartbeat the kiss became something much more primal and urgent. Sebastian struggled to hold back, but soon they were hurtling towards the brink of losing all control, faster than anything he'd experienced before.

Suddenly Aneesa wrenched her mouth away and surged back in Sebastian's arms, cheeks high with colour. He could feel the jerky breaths making her chest rise and fall enticingly, and he knew that she had no idea how utterly sensual she was...and to think that her husband would not have appreciated *this*?

As he stood on the precipice of making a momentous decision—for there was no way he was letting Aneesa leave him now—he felt acutely vulnerable. For the first time someone stood before him and didn't see the infamous Sebastian Wolfe of the scandalous Wolfe family. Nor the multimillionaire. She didn't know his history. She had no expectation of him.

It had been a long time since anyone had shown any vulnerability in front of him. Women wanted him because he presented a pleasing physical package but more for his link to notoriety and his huge fortune.

Even his own mother hadn't recognised him as her firstborn son since he'd been a child, due to her debilitating mental illness. She still, to this day, whenever she saw him, assumed he was her beloved Nathaniel, Sebastian's younger and only full-blood brother. The fact that she didn't recognise his brother either and hadn't for years, despite her obsession with him, offered little comfort. Sebastian had ceased to exist for her long ago.

He'd seen his mother only two days before, in the UK, and even though he expected nothing less after all these years, it still hurt each time to be reminded that she'd chosen to favour another over him.

So to have this woman look at him now and really see *him*, and want him for just who he was as a man, as Sebastian, was heady. For a long time desire had been largely an intellectual thing for him; he couldn't remember the last time he'd responded with such base carnality to any woman.

His hands tightened fractionally on her waist and to his intense satisfaction he saw her eyes dilate and the pulse at the base of her throat beat frantically. Her cheeks were still flushed. He had to bite back a groan of pure need. He took a breath and surprised himself by saying, 'I don't know you…yet I feel as if I've known you forever.…'

Aneesa melted inside and felt a tremor run through her. She couldn't break her gaze from his and just said huskily, 'I know…me too. It's…crazy.'

He lifted a hand to twine a loose tendril of long glossy hair around a finger and tugged her gently towards him. Aneesa all but fell back into his arms, and looked up, helpless to resist this vortex that was sucking them under.

His eyes were mesmerising, hypnotising. So when he said, 'I'd like you to stay with me tonight…let me give you the experience you've been denied…' her heart stopped for an infinitesimal moment.

CHAPTER THREE

ANEESA could barely breathe as it was, especially with his big hand on her waist. She'd been drenched in mortification ever since she'd so boldly all but begged him to kiss her. Even now she burned. But in truth, ever since she'd seen him in the shadows earlier, on some level she'd wished for this moment, not even knowing that she'd see him again. Not even knowing what she'd really wanted. And what she wanted now, with a fierce need, was *him*.

'I…' she began, and stopped. Was she really going to do this? Just throw caution to the wind? He subtly moved her so that her body was flush with his, so that she could feel his thighs against hers through the material of their clothes. When she felt a hard ridge she blushed even fiercer.

She stalled, trying with a desperate feeling of futility to cling onto some kind of sanity. 'I don't even know you.…' An insidious suspicion struck her and she pulled back slightly. 'Do you do this often? I mean, it's easy for you to just offer to take women to bed like this?'

He quirked a smile, a devastating smile. 'I've never before met a woman and wanted her so badly that I've been aching to take her to bed within minutes of meeting her. Trust me. And trust that what's happening between us isn't usual for me on any level. Or, I think, *you.*'

Sebastian realised the import of what he was saying. It was true. He'd never been so overcome with a desire to bed a woman that he hadn't been able to take her out one night and then seduce her the next, but here now with Aneesa…there was an urgency in his body he'd never felt before. It made him feel vulnerable enough to make boundaries clear from the outset. 'What I'm proposing is that we have just this one night, where we can act on this desire. Explore it to its fullness. And you…can have your wedding night, not as you planned it…but in your own way.'

Aneesa looked at him and tried very hard to be rational. 'You're not just doing this out of pity?'

He smiled again and there was a touch of pain to it. He pulled her even closer so that now she could be in no doubt as to the extent of his arousal. She almost groaned aloud, a liquid heat invading her lower body, making her tremble.

'Does that feel like pity to you?'

She shook her head dumbly, incapable of speech.

'I wanted you from the moment I saw you arrive in that courtyard—that's the truth. Your fiancé used you to suit his own ends…but you are an extremely desirable woman.'

He was effortlessly honing in on the insecurity she'd felt about herself as a woman for as long as Jamal had avoided making love to her. 'I saw you in the shadows—I thought of you…just before I decided to run…'

His hands moved up from her waist, brushing the

sides of her breasts until he cradled her jaw, fingers tunnelling through her unravelling hair, caressing her skull.

This was right. She felt it in every bone of her body. The primal urge to mate with *this* man was almost overwhelming. She *wanted* him to be her first lover. She was meant to be here with him, tonight. And in the days and weeks to come when she would have to deal with the consequences of her actions, she would be able to hug this secret moment to herself. Tonight would be the oasis in the storm to come. This was her chance to become a woman with a man who truly desired her—*on what should have been her wedding night*—and she wanted that experience more than she'd wanted anything in her life.

'I want you to make love to me, Sebastian. Just for tonight.'

He bent his head and came closer. Aneesa's heart threatened to jump out of her chest, and just before his mouth met hers again he said, 'Just one night…'

She nodded her head. How could she explain to him that if her family found out about this on top of what she'd just done she might as well emigrate to Alaska forever? Anything beyond tonight was not an option and she knew that.

The kiss, like last time, started slow and gentle. But any restraint or gentleness fast disappeared in an escalating mutual fire of need. Aneesa blindly took Sebastian's lead and their tongues duelled in a heady dance. Her hands were on his chest, ostensibly to cling onto something solid, but now they wound up and around his neck, bringing her into even more intimate contact with his lean body.

With a muffled groan that resonated right down to her toes, Sebastian's hands slipped down her back, skimming over the curves of her waist and hips, to cup her bottom and pull her into him even more. Her breasts were flattened against his chest, nipples chafing against her tight bodice.

When she felt the thrusting force of his arousal at the apex of her legs she broke away, breathing harshly.

Sebastian's face was flushed, eyes glittering a dark blue. Throatily he said, 'Aneesa, I know what we just said, but if you want to stop…just say the word.'

Everything in her rejected that thought. She'd been living behind a façade of her own making for so long and suddenly things felt clear and bright for the first time in her life. She shook her head fiercely. 'No…I don't want you to stop. Don't ever stop.'

In a tender gesture that made her heart flutter, he smoothed back some hair from her brow. 'Why don't we go somewhere more comfortable?'

She nodded and, taking her hand, Sebastian led her towards the bedrooms. That clarity hit Aneesa as they walked through the quiet and darkened suite—the magnitude of what she was about to do…and yet she knew this was what she wanted.

In all honesty she had no idea what the immediate future held for her now, and *this* moment in time was something she had control over. Sebastian pushed open a door and they stepped in. Aneesa saw a huge room with floor-to-ceiling windows which looked out over a glittering night-time Mumbai. And then she saw the massive bed in the middle of the room. Her heart tripped once and then took up an unsteady beat.

He let her go briefly to turn on a lamp and it threw

out a seductively low light, bathing the room in shadows and burnishing Sebastian with a kind of golden glow. Before she had time to think too much he was back, right in front of her and leading her close to the bed.

Gently he turned her around so that her back was to his chest. She felt him start to unbraid her hair and she dropped her head with a delicious shiver skating up her spine. Her hair fell in a sleek black curtain to just between her shoulder blades.

Then he took the ornately decorated end of the sari that was wound up and over her shoulder and pulled it away where it fell to drape over her arm. She could feel the air caress her bare skin where her bodice was revealed and cut very low. She heard Sebastian's indrawn breath and then felt his knuckles gliding over her skin. She shivered and said with a tiny moan, 'Sebastian…' his name dropping effortlessly from her mouth as if she'd been saying it all her life.

He pulled her hair over one shoulder and pressed a kiss to the place where her shoulder met her neck and she realised that he was undoing the tiny fastenings holding her bodice together. It was loose in seconds and he pushed it apart to bare her back completely.

Aneesa couldn't and didn't want to stop him when from behind her he pushed her top down her arms until it fell to the floor along with the end of her sari. She was naked from the waist up and Sebastian came right up behind her and snaked his hands around her, trailing them with infinite slowness up over her belly to the underside of her breasts.

Eyes closed, Aneesa beseeched him silently and couldn't stop the convulsive shiver when his hands came up and cupped her breasts fully, trapping her nipples between his fingers. She arched her back which pressed her bottom into him and she could feel his arousal, rock hard and insistent.

Little moans were coming from somewhere as Sebastian kneaded her breasts, making her nipples stand even more erect, and she only realised then that *she* was the one making the sounds.

With a smooth move he finally turned her around to face him and Aneesa bit her lip, knowing she should be feeling embarrassed or shy, but unable to drum up anything other than intense need. Sebastian's eyes dropped to take in her breasts and down to where her hips flared out from a small waist.

Almost reverently he touched her curves. 'You're so beautiful, like nothing I've ever seen before....'

He slowly started to unravel the sari from around her waist, until he reached to where it was tucked into her underskirt. With a flick the voluminous material fell to the floor and he was undoing the catch on the skirt so that it, too, fell. Aneesa stood before him now, naked but for a gold chain around her waist.

She flushed hotly and felt the need to explain. 'The women who got me ready had no idea that I wouldn't be indulging in a traditional wedding night with my husband. They didn't know that this would have been... wasted on him.'

Sebastian's eyes lifted and caught hers, his jaw clenched. 'Well, it's not wasted on me—it is an honour for me to see you uncovered like this.'

Absurdly Aneesa felt tears threaten. But then Sebastian was bending down to her feet where he lifted first one foot and then the other to take off her shoes. Taking each foot in his hand, he kissed where the henna tattoo snaked up in an ornate design to above her ankles.

And then he took her hands and pressed kisses into each hennaed palm. From where he was, crouched before her, he slowly slid his hands up her legs, first one and then the other, until she had to lean on his shoulders because she was afraid she might fall.

Her long hair slipped over one shoulder as she looked down. With one hand cupping her bottom Sebastian slid his other hand up between her legs, gently encouraging her to part them for him. Aneesa's heart stopped dead and her breath caught in her throat as those long fingers delved through her dark curls to her most intimate place, stroking along plump moistness where she could feel a pulse throb.

Her legs wobbled, knees threatening to give out, as she gasped, 'Sebastian…' Her hands tightened on his shoulders, as he seemed to effortlessly know just what to do to stoke her desire higher and higher. Her belly was clenched, her skin tingling all over and her head felt like it might explode.

'It's…too much…' *It's not enough!* The contradictory thoughts rang in her head.

She wanted him to stop and never to stop, and it was overwhelming. She nearly cried out when he took his hand away and stood again. He pressed a hot kiss against her mouth and said, 'Sorry…we'll take it slower…'

Aneesa was immediately contrite. 'No…I mean, I don't know…I just—'

He shushed her with a finger to her lips. 'You don't

have to say anything…it's OK. This is just the beginning.'

And then he started to strip, making her mind go blank. His shirt came off to reveal that stunningly beautiful chest again and then his hands were on his trousers. Helplessly her eyes dropped and she watched in fascination as he pulled them down over lean hips and dropped them to the floor. He stood before her, naked except for a pair of briefs and they bulged with his powerful arousal.

When he pulled them down too, lights exploded behind Aneesa's eyes to see him revealed in all his glory, massively aroused, and she longed to reach out and explore.

As if he'd heard her wanton thought, he said huskily, 'Touch me, Aneesa.'

Too scared to touch him where she really wanted, hesitantly she lifted her gaze and then reached out to run her hands over his chest, feeling how satin smooth his skin was under the light covering of hair. She scraped his blunt nipples with her nails, exulting in his indrawn breath and the hiss between his teeth.

And then because it was too hard not to, her gaze dropped again to take in that intimidating arousal which looked as if it had grown even bigger. Tentatively she reached out to touch him. His penis jerked and she bit her lip, reaching out again this time to wrap her hand around him.

She had a sudden memory of giggling over the *Kama Sutra* when she was in her teens with friends, when hilarity would disguise their genuine fascination with the explicit pictures they saw. She'd always felt slightly guilty by how fascinating the pictures had been to her, and when on a school trip they'd visited the sacred temples of Khajuraho, famous for their erotic sculptures, she'd been mortified at the achy hot feeling she'd felt in her belly after inspecting them, thinking that there must be something wrong with her.

But now Aneesa followed a feminine instinct as old as time and she bent down and took him in her mouth. He tasted salty and musky and her belly clenched with desire, but Sebastian was pulling her back up and she could see the fierce slash of colour across his cheeks and his eyes burning.

'Stop…that's enough for now. I won't be able to go slowly if you keep doing that.…'

When he'd seen her hennaed hand encircle him and felt the wet touch of her tongue, Sebastian had feared for his control when he'd never had to worry about it before. But something about the way she'd so innocently looked at him with such blatant hunger and had then bent down, giving him an enticing view of the curve of her waist and buttocks, had nearly sent him into orbit.

He took her hand again and led her to the bed, reaching out to a drawer nearby for protection as he did. He donned it with almost indecent haste and gently pushed her back onto the bed. Seeing her laid there, all curves, peaks and dark dips and hollows, he had to curb an animalistic instinct to brand this woman as his in the most primal way. All sense of urbanity was a mere illusion, and he struggled to claw back control. He bent down, over her, and took her face in his hands and kissed her passionately, exulting when her hands crept around his back and she kissed him with equal fervour.

Their bodies touched from head to toe, and Aneesa

could have wept with relief when she felt Sebastian's
heavy weight over her. She could feel him thrust one
leg between hers, his hair-roughened thigh chafing
exquisitely against her soft inner thighs, his erection
between them.

Then he drew back and this time explored *her*, with a
thoroughness that had her all but melting into a puddle
on the bed. With his mouth on her breast, sucking a
hard nipple deep, and his hand between her legs, fingers stroking and exploring her hot wetness, she was all
but crying out for some elusive fulfilment she'd never
craved before.

Time and reality had been reduced to this man and
this room and this aching burgeoning feeling inside
her, so when Sebastian moved over her more fully and
settled between her legs, she instinctively opened up to
him as much as she could.

'Are you ready?'

She nodded, incapable of speech. And when she felt
his blunt head thrust into her, she held in a gasp at the
intrusive sensation. Sebastian was infinitely patient,
going so slowly that she arched her back and hips towards him, making him curse softly.

He thrust again and she felt a stinging hot pain for
a second but it was obliterated when she felt him slide
even deeper inside her, causing her to move her hips ex-
perimentally. A delicious coil of sensation was building
which was heightened when Sebastian started to move
in and out. It rose higher and higher until she was pant-
ing in his arms, head back and eyes open wide as he
took her on a journey of discovery of her own body.

She barely heard another muffled curse as his movements became more urgent and with a guttural groan

she felt him tense for a long moment before his whole body collapsed over hers.

Aneesa was still trembling on the cusp of something that felt huge and momentous, but clearly Sebastian was finished. He was slumped over her now, breathing heavily, and she felt curiously dissatisfied, but also inordinately tender, stroking his back, even as she dimly wondered if this was what all the fuss was about.

A sense of disappointment rushed through her despite her attempts to block it out—what had she hoped for after all? Singing angels and blasting trumpets? She had no experience to call on....

Sebastian lifted his head then and looked down at her. He grimaced. 'I'm sorry about that....'

Aneesa blinked up at him. He was still hard inside her and it was difficult to concentrate when they were so intimately joined. 'Sorry...for what?'

He shook his head. 'That's never happened to me before—I've never lost control like that.'

Aneesa could see the tortured expression on his face. She lifted a hand to stroke his cheek. 'It's OK...really. I wasn't sure what to expect.'

A steely thread of something made his voice husky. 'I won't let it end like this....'

'What do you...*oh*...' She trailed off as he started to move within her; by degrees she could feel him grow harder again. And suddenly that aching feeling was back and intensified, the coil of tension building to such an extent that it made Aneesa want to cry out. Every cell in her body strained to reach the pinnacle.

Sebastian was remorseless and relentless, stoking the fire inside her higher and higher until her legs wrapped around his back and her hips were moving restlessly beneath him, searching desperately for *something*.

He bent his head and drew one nipple into his mouth, sucking fiercely just at the moment that every nerve in Aneesa's body stretched taut and sang out with exquisite pleasure. When Sebastian thrust one more time, she reached the elusive peak and after a heart-stopping moment of sensation so intense it bordered on being painful, she fell down and down into another world of such acute pleasures that she cried out as she fell.

She could feel her body clenching around Sebastian's thick shaft and only then did he thrust again and, with a shout, joined her in her delicious descent, a flood of warm release within her making Aneesa want to clench her legs tight around Sebastian and never let him go.

This time she couldn't speak or rationalise anything. All she knew was that singing angels and blasting trumpets would have been a pathetic accompaniment to what had just happened. Because it had surpassed anything she might have ever tried to imagine.

A delicious feeling of satiety coursed through her body, defying description. She had an intense desire to stay joined with Sebastian. When he drew back slightly and tried to pull away she went with him. He gave a dark chuckle, and when he pulled away again, Aneesa dropped her legs and let him go, even though the desolate feeling nearly stunned her with its power.

She couldn't look at him; she was too overwhelmed with what had just happened. Her skin tingled all over and her blood flowed thick and heavy in her veins. He drew her into his side in a possessive embrace, and with one powerful leg flung over hers, Aneesa fell into a deep and exhausted slumber.

She woke a couple of hours later to see nothing but inky blackness and stars twinkling outside. Sebastian lay with one arm flung over her, the other stretched out in abandon. The sheet was thrown aside and Aneesa felt greedy just looking at his glorious body. The protection was gone—dimly she realised that he must have taken care of it while she slept.

She moved slightly and winced when she felt the tenderness between her legs. Carefully she moved Sebastian's arm and lifted the sheet to see that there were spots of blood on her legs.

Stealthily she got out of bed and pulled her discarded sari around her as she found the bathroom. She closed the door softly and looked at herself in the mirror and almost didn't recognise herself. Her eyes were huge and slumberous, the kohl smudged, giving her a smokily decadent appearance. Her hair was tangled and tousled over her shoulders and her mouth was swollen from Sebastian's kisses.

And her whole body felt *different*, zinging with energy and yet deliciously lethargic. Wanting to wash away the blood, she turned on the shower and stepped in, after pulling her hair in to a messy knot on her head.

Standing under the sluicing hot spray, she didn't feel an ounce of remorse for what had happened even though she knew it would shock her fans and her family to know what she'd just done. It would just have to be her own secret, something she would hug to herself for a long time, perhaps forever....

After drying herself, she let her hair down again and wrapped the sari around herself once more, in a haphazard fashion. Uncertainty gripped her just before she opened the bathroom door. What would Sebastian expect now? Should she just leave and try to get out of the hotel without anyone seeing her?

Opening the door hesitantly she saw that Sebastian was still asleep on the bed and she crept over to the window to look out over Mumbai. Suddenly an acute sense of loneliness gripped her for just a moment, as well as a feeling of loss, that tonight was going to be the last time she would see him.

Sebastian woke with a start and for a second was thoroughly disorientated. He slept so rarely that it was disconcerting to realise he *had* slept, and more soundly than he had in ages. And then he saw her, standing at the window, with her back to him and that black hair in a luxuriant tangle over her shoulders, the red-and-gold wedding sari wrapped around her naked body.

And then he felt even more disorientated; he *never* fell asleep while with a woman. He would lay awake while she slept, or he would get up and work and he would be impatient for her to wake and leave…or else he would have already left. For a secret moment he regarded Aneesa's body and an acute rush of desire stunned him with its intensity. *Never* before had he felt such hunger for a woman he'd just bedded.

She'd been a virgin.

The memory of taking her, of thrusting into her tight body, nearly had him groaning out loud, his own body already responding forcibly. And he felt a curious tightness in his chest, along with a very unwelcome sense of possessiveness. As that emotion registered he immediately diverted his thoughts back to the physical. He'd never climaxed so hard—he'd practically blacked out for a moment that second time.…

Sensing his wakefulness, Aneesa turned around and something clenched hard in Sebastian's chest to see her beauty anew. And to see the hesitation on her face. She walked towards him slowly, hands clutching her sari to her chest.

When she stood near the bed she looked at him and said huskily, 'Thank you...for tonight.'

Sebastian smiled and felt his equilibrium return as desire surged effortlessly. 'My pleasure...'

He held out an imperious hand, beckoning her to come to him. She stalled. 'Don't you want me to go?'

Sebastian in any other instance with any other woman would have answered in the affirmative but now he said a throaty, 'No. It's still the middle of the night. How far do you think you're going to get wearing a dishevelled wedding sari and looking like you've been thoroughly bedded and not by the right man?'

He saw the blush stain her cheeks and his body responded even more violently. His conscience and guilt struck him when he thought of how tight she'd been, how out of control she'd made him feel. 'Are you sore?'

She shook her head, flushing to hear it confirmed that he had noticed she was a virgin. 'No...I bled a little but I'm fine. I...want to stay too, Sebastian...I want to do that again. Is that awful?'

Her disarming honesty caught at him somewhere inside. He shook his head and reached out to grab her hand, pulling her to him. 'No, it's not awful at all. I want you too.... We have all night and if you're not too tender—'

She shook her head. 'We only have one night. I don't want to waste a minute of it.'

A curious sense of loss assailed Sebastian at her words but he blocked it out. There was no room for such emotions in his life. He sat up and started to unwind the sari from her body. She turned around and around, as he unwound it, until it fell to the floor and she was naked again, adorned with nothing except the gold waist chain and the henna tattoo.

Pulling her down onto the bed beside him, he came up on one elbow and had to take a breath at how beautiful she looked with her hair spread out around her head, and his body tightened when he caught the tantalising scent of exotic musk. When he made love to her this time it was so slow and leisurely that she was the one who lost control and came helplessly, bucking against his hand as he explored her hot wet body, and when he slid into her, he made sure that she exploded around him first, before giving in to his own all-consuming need.

When Aneesa woke next, she was the one alone in bed. She could see the tentacles of pink in the dawn sky outside and felt a helpless lurch of pain, to know that another day was dawning and her night with Sebastian was over.

Just then he emerged from the bathroom with a towel slung carelessly around his waist, his taut body gleaming, wet hair slicked back. Instantly Aneesa felt her body melting on the inside and she had to draw up the sheet over her body as if he might see the depth of the need she felt for him, even now, after what had felt like hours of lovemaking. She'd lost count of the amount of times he'd brought her to orgasm, as if he'd had to make up for the first time.

He strolled over nonchalantly and, with a small hand towel, rubbed at his short hair, making it stand up on end.

'Morning.'

Aneesa blushed. 'Morning.' She sat up, holding the sheet to her body, and looked around for her clothes, not wanting to meet Sebastian's too-inquisitive gaze right now, afraid that he might see something of the turmoil she felt. Especially when this situation was obviously something he was well used to. She could see one end of her sari on the floor near the bed and reached down to pick it up, jumping slightly when Sebastian got it for her and handed it over.

'It's probably not the best idea to wear that out of the hotel...' he said with dry humour.

Aneesa looked at him, his easy demeanour making her feel disgruntled and tetchy. 'Well, what else can I wear? I didn't exactly plan for this...'

Sebastian's eyes flashed at her tone and Aneesa said immediately, 'I'm sorry, I didn't mean to sound so... short.'

'I can ring down and have them send up some clothes for you—jeans and a jacket, something like that?'

Aneesa nodded. 'Thank you. If I can just get out without anyone spotting me I might be able to salvage something of my ruined reputation.'

Sebastian went to the phone and called down. She barely heard what he said, his words just a deep rumble, and hoped that he'd got her size right. He turned back, and feeling very exposed in the face of his supreme assuredness, Aneesa got out of the bed and clutched her sari to her body, desperately trying to cover up, which she knew was silly when this man already knew her body more intimately than she did.

She garbled something about taking a shower and fled to the bathroom. Evidently Sebastian was only too happy that the night was over and he could say goodbye to the hysterical Indian Bollywood bride who had given up her innocence with the tiniest amount of persuasion.

When the bathroom door closed behind Aneesa, Sebastian had to battle the urge to follow her in and introduce her to the delights of making love in a shower. Just the thought of the water sluicing down over those exquisite curves was enough to make him bite back a groan of need. And ultimately that's what stopped him following her in—the fact that she could bring about this lack of control so easily.

He'd just spent an entire night with a woman when he couldn't remember the last time that had happened. If ever. He had a fleeting moment of considering making her an offer to become his mistress, here in India, so that they could keep seeing each other. But that sense of vulnerability rose up again, making him feel uncomfortable. It wouldn't be right to ask Aneesa to be his mistress; she'd been innocent and she wasn't like the more experienced women he usually chose, who knew that he liked to keep things casual.

He told himself this and resolutely diverted his mind away from exploring the real reason he wouldn't be seeing her again.

When Aneesa emerged from the bathroom with her hair freshly washed and dried, she felt a little more in control. The bedroom was empty, and in a voluminous towelling robe she went to look for Sebastian, who she found in the main living area, pristine and more than a little intimidating in a dark grey suit which made his blue eyes stand out.

He was on the phone, speaking to someone in rapid-fire Spanish when she came in, and he picked up a big glossy-looking bag to hand to her. She took it, assuming it to be the clothes, and fled back to the bedroom.

In the bag she found underwear, jeans, flat shoes, a shirt and a baseball cap. She smiled at his thoughtfulness and even more when she saw a huge pair of dark glasses. When she was dressed she pulled her hair up into a ponytail and regarded herself in the mirror. She was a million miles away from the ornately decorated bride of the night before—she grimaced slightly—except for the distinctive henna tattoo on her hands.

'I got your size right....'

Aneesa whirled around to see Sebastian leaning against the door, watching her. Heat crept over her skin to think just how intimately they'd been entwined only hours before. How intimately he knew her.

'Yes, thank you...I'm afraid I've no money to pay you for the clothes at the moment, but I could arrange for some—'

He cut off her words with a slashing movement of his hand, 'Don't worry about it.' He flicked a glance at the watch on his wrist. 'I'm afraid I have to leave. I've got a meeting in twenty minutes across town.'

She tried to ignore the wrenching sensation in the pit of her belly and stammered, 'Of course, you're busy. My parents will be worried about me. I should go to them and explain.'

He quirked a brow. 'Jamal?'

Aneesa hitched up her chin. 'Jamal will be fine—he's made surviving in Bollywood into an art form and I'm sure he's already making sure he's being portrayed as the poor victim.'

Sebastian stood away from the door. 'I know a good PR person here, if you need someone to take care of you.'

Aneesa shook her head and fought the desire to say yes, as if to hold onto some tenuous link that he was holding out, but he was only being polite. 'Thanks but my agent will have someone lined up I'm sure....'

He started to walk away. 'I'll take you down to a back entrance. I've arranged for a car to be waiting for you outside, so hopefully that'll ensure you get away without being noticed.'

Aneesa nodded and put on the baseball cap. She'd transferred all of her wedding paraphernalia into the glossy bag. As much as she never wanted to see it again, she couldn't leave it behind.

So briskly that she felt a little dizzy, Sebastian led her out, and back into the service elevator which had brought her into the suite last night. All the way down to the ground floor she wondered what one said to the man with whom you'd spent all night in complete wanton abandonment.

She felt a desperate urgency rising within her and, inexplicably, tears pricked the backs of her eyes. She pulled the baseball cap down lower, as if she could hide from Sebastian.

They reached the ground floor where a discreet member of staff waited, and he led them to a back door where there was indeed a luxury saloon waiting outside. The member of staff melted away. It was just the two of them in a plain staff corridor and Aneesa took off her cap for a moment to look up at Sebastian.

She opened her mouth to speak but nothing came out. His face looked stark and expressionless. His eyes flinty blue. She had to go now or she'd crumple, and while extending her hand, she garbled out, 'Look… thank you for…everything. I don't know what I would have done if—'

'*Aneesa.*' He took her hand and pulled her to him, his eyes burning in his face now. 'You don't have to thank me. Last night was an honour for me, even if it came on the back of your ruined wedding. I'm sorry you had to go through that, but I'm not sorry about what we shared…but you know it can't go any further than this, don't you?'

Aneesa nodded and felt like she was breaking apart inside. She'd thought she'd loved Jamal but not once had he made her feel like *this*. As if on the one hand she was dying and on the other hand being reborn again every time she looked into his eyes. And God help her but she couldn't look away.

With a look of something almost savagely intent on his face, Sebastian pulled her into his body and dipped his head. She had no defence for the kiss that followed, and heard a faint moan coming from her mouth. The kiss was harsh and brutal and yet more gentle than anything she'd experienced with him in the previous cataclysmic twelve hours.

That sense of inner desperation mounted—*she was never going to see him again*—and now she kissed him back as if her life depended on it, arms wrapped tight around his neck, their bodies straining together. When they finally drew apart they were both breathing heavily and Aneesa's heart was pounding. She realised that she was clinging onto Sebastian like an octopus and took her arms down before he had to extricate himself.

With two hands on her waist he put her back and her legs felt wobbly. She bent and picked up the fallen baseball hat and put it on with trembling hands.

'Goodbye, Aneesa.'

She couldn't even look at him. 'Goodbye, Sebastian.' And before she did something stupid, like throw herself at him and beg him not to let her go, she walked swiftly to the car, where the driver jumped out to open the door for her. The windows were tinted and she didn't look back at Sebastian once.

The following morning Sebastian was getting ready to leave the hotel to return to Europe, half listening to the news on the TV, when he heard Aneesa's name and turned to see her beautiful face filling the screen.

He turned the sound up, and then had to sit down when his legs felt suspiciously weak. It looked like a press conference and Aneesa was dressed in a conservative trouser suit, shirt buttoned up, hair tied back and sleek. Her face was pale and her eyes were huge and red-rimmed.

His hand clenched into a fist on his thigh in an unconscious reaction to the thought that she'd been upset. There was a barrage of questions but an officious-looking man to her right put up a hand. 'Miss Adani is only here to read out a statement. Please, no questions.'

Sebastian could see Aneesa's throat work and her hands shake slightly as she held a piece of paper. He saw the sleeve of her jacket pulled down as far as possible over the henna tattoo and his chest felt tight.

Her voice was hesitant at first but grew stronger; he only caught snippets of what she said, he was so distracted by seeing her.

'...like to extend my profound apologies to Jamal Kapoor Khan and his family for any distress I may have caused by my actions, and also to my own family.... My reasons for not going through with the wedding are personal to me. I wish all the best for Jamal and that he will find a partner who will appreciate him far more than I ever could have. There was no third party involved in my actions—my decision was mine alone and I must live with the consequences. I would just ask for some privacy for my family at this time. Thank you...'

At that moment she looked up and straight at the camera and Sebastian felt winded all over again, as if she was looking directly at him. He had to laugh grimly at his fanciful reaction, no wonder she was a major star. She lit up the screen, even when she was at half wattage. And he felt inordinately proud of her; she'd said exactly the right things, almost implying that she'd felt she wasn't good enough for Jamal so that she'd set him free to find someone more worthy.

A discreet knock came on the door and Sebastian flinched slightly, engrossed with watching how the media were braying for Aneesa's blood as she got up and walked away with a stiff back and heavy minders crowding around her. She'd slipped huge black glasses on and the flashing lights of hundreds of cameras lit up the screen.

Quelling an almost overwhelming urge to go and

find her and pluck her out of that bloodthirsty horde, Sebastian flicked off the TV and reminded himself that she wasn't meant to be on his mind anymore. It had been one night, an interlude. And it was over. His jaw was hard as he lifted up his bag and strode to the door of the suite, not even glancing back once.

Five Weeks Later

Aneesa was exhausted as she sank into the car that was to take her home from the film studios. She had just finished shooting a cameo role in a big budget movie. A cameo role that had been handed to her on a platter following the media furore after that press conference.

To her utter shock and abject relief, the Indian people and film lovers hadn't turned on her as she'd expected and feared. Her agent's strategy had worked; they'd made it sound as if she felt she couldn't be with Jamal as she wasn't good enough for him and the public had lapped this up, putting her in the role of a romantic martyr who was setting Jamal free to find someone else. It appealed to every level of the Bollywood-crazy film fans who thrived on similar melodramatic stories in the movies.

As the public fervour rose and they'd embraced the romantic lovelorn Aneesa, Jamal hadn't had a leg to stand on. In order to save face himself he'd had to come out and humbly thank Aneesa for running out on their wedding. She was the only one who'd read the daggers in his expression. She was the only one who knew the truth behind her desire for him 'to find someone who would appreciate him for who he really was.'

It was ironic, but at this busiest point in her career,

she was turning down work and her agent couldn't understand why she wasn't signing the umpteen lucrative contracts being pushed under her nose every day now. He thought she'd lost the plot altogether.

Before, she would have signed every contract, terrified that she'd miss out on something.

Aneesa sighed deeply. But now, something fundamental had shifted inside her and she wasn't the same person anymore. She wasn't even sure if this was the life she wanted. She didn't like the person she'd become in the industry and didn't want to be seduced by that shallow world again. She'd even started to try and reach out to old friends.

Thankfully the driver didn't make conversation as she watched Mumbai pass by outside in all its teeming and hectic, colourful glory. One thing remained constant though—the fact that she couldn't forget about Sebastian. At night she woke aching for his body and touch, her dreams all of him, and by day she couldn't get his hard-boned face and intense blue eyes out of her mind. The way he'd quirked a lazy smile when he'd introduced himself. The way he'd given her the experience of a lost wedding night.

She'd believed that he either had to be married, and had indulged in a fling, or else he was a serial seducer with women all over the world. And then only today she'd nearly had a seizure when she'd seen a picture of him in the Mumbai *Times*, where he'd been named as Sebastian Wolfe, the owner of the Mumbai Grand Wolfe Hotel. It had all slid into place. *That* was why he'd been observing the wedding, and that was why he'd had the best suite in the hotel. It was also why he'd been phoned by the staff the evening she'd sought refuge and how he'd managed to get her clothes with little more than a click of his fingers, not to mention a chauffeur-driven car....

On the heels of finding out his identity and surreptitiously looking for more information about him on the Internet, she now knew for a fact that he was not married, but *was* a serial dater of beautiful women. Not to mention the fact that he owned a string of luxury hotels in practically every major city, a private island in South America and that he came from a huge sprawling family with links to a scandalous past in Britain.

The large family of seven brothers and one sister had dispersed from the family home in Buckinghamshire, each one carving out their own destiny with their chunks of the huge inherited Wolfe fortune. There was a mention of Sebastian's younger full brother Nathaniel who was a famous Hollywood actor but very little else, almost as if some kind of embargo had been placed on the information.

It had been easier to unearth gossip about Sebastian's prowess with women, much to Aneesa's disgust and humiliation. It was rumoured that he had lovers all over the world who graced his bed whenever he called, and he was never seen with a woman for more than a few dates.

When he hadn't even asked to see her again, despite his assertion that they'd only have one night, he'd obviously relegated *her* far beneath those other women, and that realisation had *hurt*. But was she really so pathetic that she would have settled for a few scraps from his table? A few furtive visits whenever he was in Mumbai? With a feeling of burning shame, she knew what her answer to that might have been.

Aneesa looked down at her hands to where the henna tattoo had just about faded away completely and wished that she could make the memory of Sebastian fade away too. And then the niggling worry that had been getting stronger rose up again, despite her efforts to push it to the back of her mind. Her period was late. Very late. She'd put it down to the turmoil of the past few weeks and reassured herself that there was no way Sebastian's condoms could have failed in their protection.

But even as she thought that, she remembered the sensation of warm release inside her and her heart started to thump ominously.

CHAPTER FOUR

'JUST make sure it's done, Alain. I don't want to hear about this problem again.' Sebastian switched off his mobile phone and had to quell the urge to call his senior hotel manager in Paris back to apologise. He'd been like a bear with a sore head for weeks now. He knew the reason why, but as the implications of this set in, Sebastian scowled, earning a quick glance from his driver through the rearview mirror. His driver knew better though, than to engage him in conversation when he was silent like this.

The city of London slid past the car, as Sebastian tried desperately not to give into the urge to think of her *again*. It was getting worse. She'd invaded his dreams ever since India, and he'd conducted video conferences with his team in Mumbai rather than go over there again. As if he couldn't even trust himself to be in the same city.

His fist clenched automatically in rejection of that thought but he ignored it. Aneesa Adani was not like the women he sought out to be his lovers. She'd been innocent, going through a traumatic time. She lived in India and had indelible roots to the place.

And she was the only woman who had managed to

somehow sneak under his guard to a place no one had reached. Ever. Not even his own family. And for that reason alone, she was danger with a capital *D*.

Sebastian had found out shortly after returning from India that his only full sibling, his younger brother Nathaniel, had seen their prodigal oldest half-brother Jacob when he had turned up at the opening night of Nathaniel's latest West End play after years of unexplained absence. Nathaniel had left the stage, which had led to a sequence of events that had forced Nathaniel to seek sanctuary from the press on Sebastian's private island.

It had sparked a revival in media interest in their scandalous family history, and in the whereabouts of his and Nathaniel's mother, something they could both have done without. While Sebastian got on with most of his siblings, even if he didn't see much of them now, his relationship with Nathaniel was his closest one, albeit largely from a distance. The relationship with his oldest half-brother, however, had been non-existent for years.

Once, Jacob had been Sebastian's only anchor in a dark and unstable world. An adored and revered older brother. By the age of ten, Sebastian had witnessed more than any child of his age should have had to, and had dealt with seeing his mother being sent to a mental institution.

He'd always been the loner out of all his siblings, a cerebral child who had struggled in isolation to comprehend the mercurial moods of their charismatic father. But at a crucial point in Sebastian's life, Jacob had left the home with no warning and no explanation, and ever since then Sebastian had had no one who'd cared enough to coax him out of himself. From that moment on, he'd become even more withdrawn.

And without the anchor of their oldest brother, all the Wolfe siblings had inevitably drifted apart. Sebastian had buried the pain of that abandonment deep inside him and had channelled all of his energy into a single-minded desire to succeed. Which he had done many times over.

Jacob's return now was precipitating a whole host of unwelcome emotions within Sebastian, and so far he'd managed to avoid meeting him. However, Sebastian had just agreed to let Nathaniel use his London hotel for his upcoming wedding, and he knew that Jacob was due to attend, so even though he had no wish to avoid the rest of his family, if Jacob was going to be there, then Sebastian was planning on being unavoidably busy for the day.

Suddenly he knew the best solution to distract him from unwelcome thoughts of Aneesa *and* his family: he would take a new lover. He didn't need to be reminded that he hadn't slept with anyone since Mumbai and in his own head vehemently denied that it was because *she'd* ruined him for anyone else. That was a ridiculous thought. Bitterness gripped him—he was his father's son. He carried William Wolfe's warped genes and his father had never found peace with one woman. So why would Sebastian suddenly buck the trend? Or, worse, feel inclined to?

He picked up his phone again and made a call to a very persistent socialite he'd met at a party some weeks before. He hadn't been interested then, but suddenly he was very interested. Almost desperate, in fact.

* * *

Aneesa sat nervously in Sebastian's London office, in awe of the plush understated luxury and the mile-high view which took in the London Eye in the near distance. Her belly was tied in knots and she felt a semi-hysterical giggle rising up to think of what else was in her belly: *a baby.* Sebastian's baby.

But then the reality of what faced her made her sober up again fast. The irony of getting pregnant on her non-wedding night, and to another man, hadn't been lost on her.

She'd known for some time now and, in that time, had developed an indelible bond with the tiny being inside her. There was no question, but she was having this baby, no matter what the fallout, and she'd known well that her career most likely wouldn't survive this. The equanimity she'd felt when faced with that prospect told her that she'd definitely started to move on from the Bollywood world.

And in the past two weeks her suspicions had been proved right and events had led her here, to Sebastian's office in London. She'd tried the hotel in Mumbai first, but they'd told her that Sebastian had no immediate plans to come back to India. Aneesa had quashed the suspicion that that was because of *her.* Surely he couldn't want to avoid her that badly? Even now that thought made her feel ill inside. And then...with everything that had happened at home, she'd had no real choice but to leave India, so she'd taken the opportunity to come to England and tell Sebastian face to face.

A noise outside and the familiarly deep rumble of a voice made her heart stop. A clammy sweat broke out over her skin. The door opened and she sat frozen on the couch as she watched the tall and achingly familiar figure of Sebastian stride in.

He didn't see her at first as her seat was partially hidden behind the door but as it swung shut she gathered all her courage and stood.

'Sebastian.'

That distinctively husky voice, the beguiling hint of an accent, had Sebastian whirling round, half terrified his dreams were haunting him by day now. And when he saw her, he reeled.

Aneesa gripped her hands tight together. Sebastian looked as if she'd just driven a stake through his belly. For an awful heart-stopping moment she thought he didn't even recognise her. But before she could say anything he issued a curt, 'How did you get in this time? Did you materialise through another service elevator?'

Hurt lanced her and Aneesa fought not to quail at the clear evidence of his hostile reaction to seeing her. 'No.' She flushed. 'The security guard downstairs recognised me and when I explained I was looking for you he took me up here to wait. There was no one outside so he brought me straight in.'

She didn't want to go into the way the Indian guard had balked at the notion of someone like her waiting for Sebastian anywhere other than his office. Aneesa had surmised grimly that the news of her infamy hadn't reached as far as England yet. Blistering energy crackled off Sebastian for a long moment and Aneesa had to consciously not let her eyes drop and take in that gorgeous body, but even peripherally she could see the way his exquisite suit hugged his powerful frame. Heat washed through her and her belly tightened.

Abruptly Sebastian relaxed visibly and ran a hand through his hair which Aneesa noticed had grown longer since she had last seen him. She could see now that he looked slightly weary, with faint lines around his mouth and eyes that she hadn't noticed before. And it looked as though he'd lost weight.

'I'm sorry, there was no need for me to be so rude. It's just…a bit of a shock to see you here. That's all.' Even now Sebastian had to wonder if he was going mad—was he imagining this? *Had* he inherited his mother's mental instability?

Immediately Aneesa felt obliged to rush and explain. 'I know we agreed that it would be one night only, that we'd never see each other again…'

She drove down the hurt again at his reaction and steeled herself. Her life was about taking responsibility now and she had to keep going. 'But I've come to tell you something.'

He looked at her, head back. Aneesa's heart was racing. He wasn't making this easy for her at all. She took a deep breath and then said in a rush before she could lose her nerve, 'I've come to let you know that I'm pregnant…with your baby.'

Sebastian blinked. Aneesa didn't disappear. She was still there, in front of him, flesh and blood. In tight jeans and a T-shirt, a soft figure-hugging leather jacket. Her hair down and her face pale and devoid of make-up. Almond-shaped eyes huge. And utterly, utterly beautiful. For a second he'd thought she was about to say that she'd come because she hadn't been able to forget about him, and even amidst the shock he felt a bubbling up of something which felt suspiciously like joy.

And then what she *had* said impacted on him, like a delayed reaction.

His eyes narrowed, he cracked out, 'Pregnant? You're pregnant, and it's mine?'

Aneesa looked hesitant. Unsure. And Sebastian had to drive down the immediate need to reassure her. This was too huge. Well-ingrained cynicism surged. He asked again when Aneesa didn't respond immediately. 'Is it mine?'

'Well, of course it's yours…you're the only…' She faltered. 'I've not been with anyone else.'

On a reflex Sebastian's eyes dropped to Aneesa's waistline where there was only the slightest hint of a belly. Which could be nothing, or could be something. *His baby.* He felt dizzy. He sought refuge in rising anger which he knew had something to do with the fact that she hadn't just made this trip because she couldn't forget him and wanted to see him again.

The anger rose up, directed at her now for being here, and invading his peace, when he had so recently been castigating her for that. A small voice mocked him: *Peace? Since when have you had peace in your life?* Like a coward, Sebastian ignored the memory of the long minutes he'd slept in Aneesa's company that night.…

'I used condoms.' His voice was icy cold.

Aneesa flushed; imperceptibly her chin hitched up. 'I know. But it must have… Something must have happened. This *is* your baby—why would I come all the way here if it wasn't? Believe me, this was as much of a shock to me as it is to you.'

Sebastian crossed his arms. Aneesa shivered slightly. 'Did you decide to pass off your child as mine once you found out about the Wolfe family fortune? Or did you know who I was all along? It seems awfully coincidental now that you just happened to find your way to my suite that night. Perhaps like today, an eager fan let you in so you could stage your dramatics?'

All Sebastian was aware of was the need to drive Aneesa and her terrifying news back. Her mouth was open on a gasp as she took in his words, the colour leaching from her face, and he had a flash of memory at just how distraught she'd been, that look they'd shared at her wedding when she'd reminded him of a panicked and trapped animal being led to its doom.

He also had a memory of the moment when they'd made love and he'd all but blacked out… Possibly in that moment, the protection had failed. And even as he thought that, a grim cold certainty lodged in his belly. Aneesa was pale and stunned-looking. He knew she was an actress, but no one could fake *this*.

But it was too late. She was picking up her bag and heading for the door, back rigid.

She had her hand on the doorknob and she turned around, her face white. 'That is a despicable thing to say.' Her English got more stilted. 'I was in ignorance of who you were until five weeks after you'd left— believe it or not, I had other things on my mind. And I only found out because I saw you in a paper. If this is the way you react to finding out you're going to be a father, then I wish I'd remained in ignorant bliss.'

She finished caustically. 'And you can take your Wolfe fortune and jump off the London Eye for all I care!'

With that she opened the door and swept out with all the hauteur of a queen. Sebastian could hear his

PA's startled exclamation as this exotic beauty emerged from his office. He was stunned for a second too, and then what finally galvanised him were her words: *you're going to be a father*. And just like that, the reality of what she was saying sank in and he couldn't hide behind the anger any more.

Aneesa stood at the lift and pressed the button again impatiently; she was *not* going to cry, she was *not* going to cry. Even though her throat ached and the backs of her eyes burned. She could have laughed at her brave assertion just now *that she'd had other things on her mind*, when he'd been on her mind morning, noon and night.

He didn't believe that the baby was his, and she truly hadn't expected that. But her naivety mocked her. He must have women coming out of the rafters claiming to have his children. And he believed that she'd deliberately seduced him? That hurt the most. He'd tainted their magical night with cynicism. He was hard and unforgiving and not at all like the man she remembered.

The lift bell pinged just as she felt her arm taken in a strong grip. A familiar and evocative scent tickled her nostrils. The doors opened and she tried to pull free to step in, but couldn't.

'Don't go.' His deep voice sent a quiver through her body. 'Please. Forgive me for what I just said.'

She looked up at him and her legs went wobbly when she registered his closeness, and saw those eyes up close again. His hand warm on her arm through her jacket.

'I'm sorry, I shouldn't have said…what I just said. It was unforgivable.'

The ache in Aneesa's throat diminished. 'Yes, it was.

I just wanted to let you know—I felt you deserved that much.'

He tugged her arm gently. 'Come back inside. You look like you could do with a cup of tea.'

Reluctantly Aneesa let herself be guided back through to his office, barely hearing him ask his middle-aged PA for some tea and informing her that he shouldn't be disturbed for the rest of the afternoon.

When the tea was brought in, Aneesa sat on the couch, with Sebastian in a chair opposite her, for all the world now as if they were acquaintances catching up in civilised surroundings and not as if a bomb had just been dropped into the room, into their lives. Stalling, she took a sip of hot tea, relishing its calming heat.

'When did you arrive?'

She looked at Sebastian and hated the little lurch her heart gave. She knew it would be so, so dangerous to harbour feelings for him. He might have apologised but he certainly wasn't showing an inkling of the man she'd met that night who had been so tender and considerate.

She put the cup down. 'This afternoon. I came straight from the airport.' She looked him in the eye and steeled herself. 'The honeymoon period I had with the media after the wedding disaster is over.'

His eyes narrowed, brows snapped together. 'What are you talking about?'

Aneesa's hands twisted in her lap. 'Jamal and his boyfriend broke up and as a form of revenge his now ex-boyfriend outed him in the papers.' She took a breath. 'And on pretty much the same day, a nurse from the clinic I'd gone to for confirmation of the pregnancy leaked the news to the press for a sum of money.'

Her mouth twisted. 'The reality that I must have slept with someone other than Jamal close to the wedding was too much for the public to take. It would appear that they can take the news of Jamal being gay better than they can take the news of me becoming a single mother.'

Something in Sebastian's gut clenched. 'Is that what you want?'

No! Aneesa wanted to scream, but she just shrugged nonchalantly, avoiding Sebastian's eye. 'This wasn't meant to happen. But I want this baby and if I have to do it on my own, then so be it.'

'You won't be on your own. I'll be in the baby's life too,' Sebastian said gruffly, everything in him rejecting the notion of Aneesa and his child being alone. However, he didn't want to look too deeply into how that would work, when the very idea of anything like marriage or a long-term relationship was anathema to him. He'd been poisoned against that halcyon image since he had been a child. Nothing he'd experienced had demonstrated any kind of normal functioning relationship.

Aneesa dipped her head slightly. 'Thank you for that, but I really don't expect anything from you.'

'Where are you planning on staying while you're here?'

Aneesa flushed. She didn't want to reveal just how broke she was now. Or how she hadn't really stopped to think beyond escaping the media storm at home and feeling compelled to come and tell Sebastian face to face. She hated to think that Sebastian would feel obliged to take her in. She prevaricated. 'I…I hadn't really organised anything but I'm sure I can find somewhere this afternoon.' Worry knotted her belly; she knew she wouldn't last long in a hotel.

'I'd offer you a room in my Grand Wolfe Hotel but it's booked out for a private function this week and weekend....'

Aneesa tried to wave his suggestion away; just the thought of the cost of a room at one of his hotels made her feel nauseous. Her life had changed so much in such a short space of time, before she wouldn't have even questioned the cost of such accommodation, and would have simply taken it for granted.

She hitched up her chin again in a way that Sebastian was beginning to recognise. 'I'll find somewhere to stay…figure something out, get a job somewhere…I'm really just taking it one day at a time at the moment.'

Suddenly restless, Sebastian stood and raked a hand through his hair, pacing back and forth. The news of his impending fatherhood was making him feel numb. He couldn't process it and said distractedly, 'It's not just your responsibility now, it's mine too. There were two of us there that night, and I didn't make sure you were adequately protected.'

He didn't see the colour flare in Aneesa's pale cheeks; he only remembered the heart-stopping urgency of desire that had led him into the most frantic coupling of his life. Willing down the images with an effort, he turned back to face Aneesa. 'You can stay with me. I can't have you wandering around looking for accommodation when I have a perfectly spacious apartment. I'll call my driver round and take you there now.'

Aneesa stood, relief mixed with trepidation warring inside her. 'Are you sure? I don't want to upset your routine. I know you must be busy. I can go to a coffee shop, wait until you finish work…'

Sebastian quirked a small harsh smile and decided not to tell her how he'd quite regularly work till midnight before going home only to toss and turn, or else head out and pound the pavements for hours, coming back exhausted at dawn. And then he remembered something and the smile faded. 'No, really, it's fine. I have to head home soon anyway as I'm going out this evening.'

Sebastian started to usher Aneesa out of the office and she bit back the urge to ask him if it was a date. He could even have a girlfriend—how would she know? Or perhaps he was meeting his London mistress? Stomach roiling, they picked up her bags from the overexcited security guard downstairs, who had somehow in the interim managed to get some DVDs of Aneesa's movies. She autographed them, and posed for a photograph with the man wearing a fixed smile, and then was being ushered into the back of Sebastian's luxury car with tinted windows.

Sitting in the back, listening to Sebastian take a call on his phone, he was a million miles from the man she'd met that night in Mumbai, and when she looked back on it now, it all seemed like a flimsy mirage, because this man was acting as if he wouldn't kiss her again if his life depended on it.

'…and then Daddy said that I simply must have the house in Holland Park, and I said…'

Sebastian let the woman's irritating voice tune in and out, nodding occasionally to signal his interest when really he had no more interest in the anaemic blonde sitting opposite him than he would in the overweight maître d' who'd shown them to the table. Which was strange as up until recently blondes had been his preference—the cooler, the better. He scowled inwardly. Until he'd met an exotic Indian princess.

It had been too late this afternoon to cancel the date and some rogue part of him had wanted to keep it, make boundaries clear with Aneesa. But he hadn't been able to get the wounded bruised look from her eyes out of his head all evening. Her eyes were so damn expressive. And beautiful.

She'd meekly followed him around his state-of-the-art penthouse apartment with its stunning views of London and had lightly asked, 'Always the penthouse?'

And he'd answered glibly, 'It's the best.' And had winced at how crass that sounded.

His housekeeper, Daniel, a man in his fifties who Sebastian would trust with his life, had immediately taken Aneesa under his wing, and when Sebastian had been leaving, she'd been sitting in the kitchen on a high stool, looking about sixteen and discussing Indian curry recipes.

As his focus came back into the exclusive restaurant, Sebastian felt suddenly impatient. He cut abruptly across the woman, whose name he struggled to recall. 'I'm sorry but I'm afraid I'll have to go...'

Her lipsticked mouth opened and closed, making a coil of disgust settle in Sebastian's belly when he remembered another mouth, with naturally red lips, full and infinitely more kissable. His body tightened in response.

He hustled them out of the restaurant, ignoring her

protests, and bundled her into a taxi, and with that impatience rising he got into a taxi himself and headed home. When he got to his building, he strode straight past the concierge and into the lift.

And it was only when he went in his front door and let the quiet of the apartment wash over him did he realise how fast his heart was hammering. He prowled silently to the bedroom he'd shown Aneesa to earlier and pushed open the door. A bedside lamp threw out a halo of light over where she had fallen asleep half sitting up in the bed. A book lay open by her side and Sebastian went over and picked it up, only noticing then what the title was: *What to Expect When You're Expecting.*

With a funny feeling in his belly he put it down and looked at Aneesa. Her long lashes were fanned out, casting shadows on her cheeks. He'd only met her once before, as cataclysmic as that meeting had been, and yet, he felt as if he'd known her forever. Exactly as he'd told her that night, like a gauche teenager.

Seeing her again, having her here, a physical reality in his home, the knowledge that she was *pregnant* was a shock to his system that was only now beginning to wear off. And on the heels of that was a disturbing build-up of ambiguous emotions he didn't want to look at.

Physically he wanted her with a fierceness that scared him. And yet he knew if he so much as touched her, a storm would be unleashed. A storm he didn't want to deal with. A surge of emotion made his gut clench even though he denied it furiously. He couldn't afford to forget that if she wasn't pregnant, she wouldn't be here now. *She wouldn't have come just because she wanted to.* He wouldn't have to be dealing with this. His conscience pricked—tonight's date would have still been a disaster, even without Aneesa's arrival. The truth hurt; he'd been dealing with her presence since that night in Mumbai....

His eyes drifted down, and feeling like a voyeur but unable to stop himself, he could see that the soft rise and fall of the swells of her breasts under her T-shirt looked fuller. Was that because of the baby? Suddenly the thought of watching Aneesa's body ripen with his child made him feel alternately euphoric and claustrophobic.

He backed away and out of the room again and it was only when he was fighting his usual losing battle with sleep some time later did he register his dominant emotion when he'd returned home to find her asleep in bed; it had been *relief.* To Sebastian's disgust, when he closed his eyes, all he could see was an image of storm clouds threatening over every horizon.

The following morning, when Sebastian returned from his regular six-mile run, the sun was rising in earnest and he was disconcerted to find Aneesa up and pottering about the kitchen. Her hair was tied back in a high ponytail and she was wearing sweatpants and a long-sleeved T-shirt.

Hardly out of breath, Sebastian said, 'You're up early.'

Aneesa whirled around, colour flooding her cheeks, and it made inexplicable satisfaction course through Sebastian. She recovered swiftly though; he could see that faint reserve return.

'I'm always up around dawn to do my meditation

and yoga practice.' She looked at him steadily. 'Will that bother you?'

Sebastian shook his head and tried to ignore the vivid mental images flooding his brain of Aneesa doing stretches. He brushed past her and her fresh scent teased his nostrils. Almost angrily he yanked out the coffee beans to make fresh coffee.

Hesitantly Aneesa asked, 'Are you sure you don't mind? You seem a little...edgy.'

Sebastian gritted his teeth. 'I'm sure. I'm just not used to living with someone, that's all. Was there something you were looking for here?'

Now she shook her head, wide eyed. 'No, I just made some herbal tea, which Daniel got for me yesterday.'

She was standing by the solid-wood island, sipping her tea. There was feet separating them and yet Sebastian could feel sweat breaking out on his brow, which got worse when she asked politely, 'Did you have a nice dinner last night?'

No! Sebastian wanted to shout, but calmed himself down and said smoothly, 'Lovely, thank you—pleasant food and pleasant company.'

Now why had he said that when it had been anything but? Feeling seriously disgruntled he left the coffee and muttered something about taking a shower and walked out of the kitchen.

Aneesa watched Sebastian leave, taking his intense force field of energy with him, and sagged back against the counter. She put a hand on her belly and tried to breathe deep to calm her thundering heart. Surely this intense physical reaction every time she saw him couldn't be good for the baby? But he'd smelt so *good*, of musky sweat and pure man. He'd obviously been out jogging, dressed in sweats like her and a T-shirt which had been all but welded to his damp chest.

If it hadn't been for Daniel distracting her yesterday evening and making her feel thoroughly at home, she was afraid she would have let Sebastian see exactly how affected she'd been by watching him go out for the evening, dressed in a black suit and crisp white shirt. His subtle aftershave had told her, with a woman's intuition, that he'd most definitely been going on a date.

And yet what could she say or do? He patently didn't welcome her presence, baby or no baby. He had a life; he must have lovers. He'd been very clear that night in Mumbai that he didn't want anything more to do with her. And yet here she was.

A wave of loneliness and homesickness washed over her and she escaped into her bedroom before Sebastian could come back and see her distress.

After pacing impatiently in the main drawing room of the apartment for about an hour, Sebastian looked at his watch for the umpteenth time. *Where* was she? He needed to speak to her before he went out to work but there was no sign of her.

Finally he went to her room and knocked lightly on her door. Hearing nothing he went in and saw her sitting cross-legged in the middle of the room, eyes closed, back straight and palms facing up resting on her knees. She looked so serene and peaceful that Sebastian tried to creep back out again but just then her eyes opened. In a second she'd got to her feet in one graceful motion. 'Was there something…?

'Just what do you expect to happen here?' The words came out baldly and Sebastian winced inwardly. He seemed to lose any ability to be suave and smooth around this woman.

She frowned. 'What do you mean?'

He gritted his jaw. 'What I mean is that I hope you haven't come here with some notion that we can happily play house just because we have a baby coming. Because that scenario is not something I am interested in.'

Anger bubbled within Aneesa, and something more emotional that she valiantly tried to keep down. A dark flush rose into her pale cheeks; her eyes flashed. 'You're afraid that I've got some plan up my sleeve to get you to marry me and make an honest woman of me?'

Sebastian threw out a hand. 'How would I know? Isn't that what every woman wants?'

Aneesa's hands clenched to fists at her sides, the calming benefits of the past half-hour of meditation wasted. 'Not this woman. After what I have been through recently, marriage or getting married is the last thing on my mind, believe me. To be perfectly frank, I don't think I *ever* want to get married. It's obvious that this is all a massive inconvenience to you. I can leave today, it's no problem. The last thing I want to do is cramp your bachelor lifestyle.'

Anger blurring her vision now, Aneesa went to her suitcase which was still half unpacked. She hauled it to the bed and with hands shaking started to throw things in. 'I've told you about the baby, and that's enough. Now I should leave and let you get on with your life. I can let you know when the baby is born and perhaps we can come to some arrangement where you can visit when you want. That's if you're interested.'

She stopped for a moment, her chest heaving and her eyes blurring with tears this time.

'And where exactly are you going to go?'

Sebastian's voice came from much closer and was so unexpectedly gentle that, to her horror, tears started to fall. She dashed them away angrily. 'I don't know. I'll think of something. This is one of the biggest cities in the world—I'm sure I can find somewhere. I should never have bothered you.'

She felt his hands on her shoulders and then she was being pulled around. Sebastian handed her a handkerchief. He led her over to the bed to sit down. She pulled back from him, her breath still jerky. 'I really didn't think beyond getting out of India so that the story could die down. I don't have some dastardly plan to trap you in a marriage or a relationship you clearly don't want.'

She shrugged one slim shoulder and looked at him. 'I felt I owed it to you to at least tell you face to face. Do you think I would have asked for any of this in a million years if given a choice?'

Aneesa bit her lip before continuing. 'By the time I was getting married, my father's business was almost bankrupt. The wedding was a huge burden on him financially. I've paid him back every penny and made him sell the apartment he bought in Juhu as part of my dowry. I couldn't stay and have them suffer the media on their doorstep every day. At least now they have some peace and my father is back on his feet and can provide for the rest of my family again. My career is over and I'm going to have to start all over again. But right now that's the least of my worries.'

She felt fierce when she said, 'But I don't regret what happened between us that night and I don't regret becoming pregnant. This child will be loved, and wanted. And I'm not telling you this because I want your money. I can look after myself and I'll look for somewhere else to stay. I'm sure I can get a job....'

A look of stoic determination came into her eyes. 'I could work here for my board?'

Something about the way she'd asserted that their child would be *wanted* struck Sebastian deep down inside. The reality was sinking in more and more by now and he knew that despite his own woeful upbringing, he, too, wanted any child of his to have a stable and loving environment. However that might be achieved.

Drily he asked, 'When was the last time you did laundry or washed dishes or even shopped?'

Aneesa flushed brick-red. 'Once I might have been like that, but not any more. I'm a fast learner and I don't mind a bit of hard work.'

Something within Sebastian twisted at her innate pride and how far she'd fallen from her Bollywood princess pedestal. She wasn't at all like the vacuous spoilt woman he'd assumed her to be on her wedding day. He couldn't believe though that she wasn't resenting her abrupt fall from grace, even if she didn't show it.

She went on with a rush. 'Look—I meant everything I've just said. You just happen to be the father of this baby. I really don't expect anything from you at all.'

Sebastian tried to ignore the effect her huge shimmering eyes were having on his equilibrium. How could he feel dizzy sitting down?

He focused with effort. 'Quite apart from the fact that you've already got Daniel wrapped around your finger, he would have a fit to see you treading on his turf. You're welcome to stay for as long as you need.'

He quirked a smile and ran a hand through his hair, 'Hell…we're having a baby.' His smile faded. 'It's just going to take me a while to absorb that. I'm not used to sharing my space.…'

'I'll stay out of your way.'

Sebastian shook his head and took the handkerchief out of her hand to wipe at a stray tear on her cheek. 'No…it's not your problem. It's my problem to deal with. This is your home now as much as mine. And we need to look into booking you in with a doctor and setting up appointments.'

'I can do all that, you're busy.'

Sebastian shook his head. 'I'll have my PA do some research.'

His hand was cupping her jaw now, and Aneesa had stopped breathing. Her body was reacting, tightening, melting, *remembering*. For a second she thought she saw an answering heat in Sebastian's eyes but then he got up and moved away, becoming brisk. Cold again.

'I've got a meeting in Paris this afternoon. I'll be back late tonight, but as it's the weekend tomorrow I'll be off so we can discuss doctors and hospitals.' He frowned now. 'How long are you intending to stay?'

Aneesa's heart thumped to think that he might actually care, which was ridiculous. 'Perhaps a couple of months? Until the scandal dies down at home—my family will be worried if I stay away for too long.'

Sebastian shrugged, a dart of emotion slicing through him at her easy mention of family. 'Like I said, you're welcome for as long as you want.'

And then he was gone. Aneesa felt slightly stunned.

She wasn't used to having emotional outbursts like that but she figured it had to be her pregnant hormones and the way Sebastian's less than ecstatic reaction to her arrival made her feel so vulnerable. And if that insouciant shrug just now was anything to go by, evidently he wasn't prepared to have much of a say in the baby's development, or birth.

Aneesa put her hand on her belly and said out loud, 'Looks like it's just going to be us, baby....'

When she got up and started to put away her things again, she resolutely pushed down the ache in her chest that told her of a very secret and treacherous desire that Sebastian's reaction to seeing her again might have been different. But reality was harsh and that was something she'd been getting a master class in recently.

CHAPTER FIVE

By Saturday evening Aneesa was worn out. She'd spent the day with Sebastian and his assistant exhaustively going through the hospitals and prenatal doctor recommendations, before finally making some choices. And while for her it was hammering the reality of her pregnancy home more and more, if anything it seemed to make Sebastian retreat further and further.

Late this afternoon he'd absented himself from discussions and gone to his study. When Aneesa had been letting his pleasant middle-aged assistant out of the apartment, the PA turned to Aneesa and confided, 'I'm very happy for you both...I've always hoped that Sebastian would—'

The older woman had stopped abruptly and blushed and then said awkwardly, 'I'm sure you don't need to hear my ramblings. Goodbye, dear.'

And she was gone, leaving Aneesa wondering what on earth she'd been about to say. She whirled around with a guilty flush on her face as if she'd been caught out when Sebastian said from behind her, 'I thought we'd stay in to eat tonight. Frankly, I'm bushed.'

Aneesa looked at him carefully. He did look tired and her heart clenched. She nodded. 'That's fine with me. I'm tired too.'

He nodded. 'Good. Daniel will have dinner ready in about an hour if you want to take a rest beforehand.'

So solicitous, so polite. The perfect host. And the father of her baby even if he didn't want to deal with it. Aneesa let out a breath when she watched Sebastian walk back into his study, and she retreated to her room where she lay on her bed looking up at the ceiling.

She wondered churlishly if Sebastian was letting a woman down tonight. If he'd had to cancel a date with the woman he'd seen the other night? Acrid emotion scared her with its intensity and she turned over and struggled to take a nap, eventually giving up with a deep sigh and having a shower instead.

She just couldn't relax knowing Sebastian was close by.

After her shower she got dressed in loose harem pants and a sleeveless vest, and left her hair down. When she went into the dining room where Daniel was just serving the starter, Sebastian stood and Aneesa felt inordinately shy. He'd obviously showered too, and his hair was wet. He was dressed in fresh jeans and a T-shirt. And looked handsome enough to make her step falter.

She cursed herself as she sat down; she was no better than a groupie with a crush.

Sebastian was grateful for Daniel's solid presence when Aneesa had appeared in the dining room. Or else he wasn't sure if he would have been able to restrain himself from smashing the heavy oak table aside and picking her up like some kind of caveman to bring back to his bedroom, to ravish her.

She was temptation incarnate. All at once deliciously curvy yet slender, silky olive skin and a tantalising glimpse of shadowy cleavage under her flimsy top. Her loose trousers merely hinted at the length of supple leg underneath and it didn't take much for him to remember how they'd felt wrapped around his back, squeezing tighter and tighter…like the muscles of her—

'Wine?'

Sebastian looked wildly at Daniel for a moment, acutely aware of Aneesa sitting down beside him, her scent on the air. He finally got out a strangled, 'Yes, red, please.' And managed to sit down again too.

Aneesa smiled widely at Daniel, hoping that her inner turmoil wasn't evident on her face. 'No wine for me, thanks. I'll just have water.'

And then they were alone. Aneesa looked anywhere but at Sebastian, and the tension mounted, until suddenly, to her utter horror and chagrin, she heard herself say with an edge to her voice, 'I hope I'm not keeping you from any commitments tonight?'

Sebastian was to her left at the head of the table, one leg touched off hers, making her blush and move her own away from the contact.

'No.' He drawled, 'No…*commitments*. I'm all yours.'

She looked at him abruptly—was he flirting with her? But even as her heart started to thump perilously, she saw that he looked far from flirtatious, more coolly stern. She let out a breath and struggled for equilibrium. 'That's good. I'd hate for you to feel like you had to entertain me.'

Sebastian had to curb his impulse to tell her exactly what he did want and at that moment Daniel returned with drinks. The thought that she might possibly be concerned about him seeing other people sent a rush of something far too disturbing to analyse through him. And when she was so close like this, it was hard to try and recall why he shouldn't be wanting her.

Aneesa was relieved to have something else to focus on and concentrated on her starter and main course as if it was the most interesting thing she'd ever encountered. Right at that moment she couldn't see herself sticking it out living in Sebastian's apartment for longer than another day, never mind a couple of months.

'So, how did you end up in Bollywood movies?'

His question took her aback and she looked at him to see that he was relaxed in his chair, watching her. Suddenly her appetite fled and she put down her knife and fork.

She took a sip of water, mouth instantly dry. She'd answered this question a million times, what was wrong with her? She just hated that she'd been so duped by such a shallow world for so long....

'I was in a shopping mall with school friends when I was seventeen. We were in our final year and a scout from a model agency spotted me.' She shrugged, feeling embarrassed. 'The next thing I knew, I was being entered for Miss India and I won...and after that the movie offers came flooding in.'

Sebastian's eyes were narrowed on her. 'You sound like you regret it.'

She shrugged again, avoiding his eye, fingers pleating the heavy linen napkin. 'I was young and spoilt. I got seduced very easily into a world that's very false.' Her mouth twisted. 'Unfortunately for a long time I believed everything people were saying to me, believed in a myth...'

'Believed that your fiancé loved you.'

Aneesa sucked in a breath and looked up into Sebastian's glittering blue gaze. He sounded so…sympathetic. She nodded. 'Yes, that too. But it was my own fault. If I hadn't become so blinded and self-absorbed I would have spotted him a mile away.'

Sebastian grimaced. 'If only it were that easy. Hindsight is a great thing.'

Aneesa half smiled and saw Sebastian's gaze drop to her mouth, making it tingle. She blushed again.

His gaze lifted. 'So…do you regret it? Do you miss it?'

Aneesa half shrugged and shook her head at the same time. 'I regret my own immaturity, but no, I don't miss it, and that's been a surprise. I've realised that it wasn't really me after all.'

She quirked a smile. 'Before I got so entranced by my own reflection I actually wanted to study medicine and had all the grade A's to back it up.' Her smile faded. 'And yet my parents stood by me and let me change course. And I repaid them by humiliating them in public in front of everyone they know.'

To her surprise Sebastian leaned forward and took the hand that was compulsively pleating the napkin. His hand was warm on hers, making tingles shoot up her arm, to her breasts where she could feel her nipples stiffen into points.

'You can't beat yourself up forever. You said yourself that you've paid them back.'

She was more than moved by the glimpse of the man she'd met that first night and terrified that he would see something of her reaction. She pulled her hand free. 'Perhaps you're right.'

She didn't see the way his jaw clenched. And to her

utter relief Daniel came in at that moment and brought tea and coffee, and cleared away the dinner plates. Sebastian served them both and then indicated that they should take their drinks into the living room.

Aneesa curled up on a big chair far from the couch where Sebastian was once again sprawled out, his long powerful body attracting her eyes more than she could resist. He'd flicked a remote and the low soothing tones of jazz flooded the room from discreet speakers. To try and distract herself from the seductive music she asked, 'So what about you? How did you end up in the hotel business?'

He cast her a glance, clearly reluctant to divulge anything. Aneesa was just regarding him steadily.

Sebastian felt a constriction in his chest. He always did, whenever anyone wanted to probe into his life, and yet…he'd just asked Aneesa about her life and was still reeling slightly from the depths she'd hidden from him, and the world.

He ran a hand through his short hair, the gesture unconscious. 'I remember being taken to a hotel with my brothers and sister for one of our birthdays when I was much smaller. It was one of the best hotels in London and I'd never seen anything like it.'

He wasn't about to reveal to Aneesa how it had made an impact on him because it had been so ordered and sleek. A world away from their chaotic home life in rambling Wolfe Manor, which had been too huge to instil any kind of order. He also wasn't going to reveal how his father had got blind drunk and the staff had discreetly whisked him away to a suite until he'd slept the excess off. And how that was the first time

Sebastian had ever seen anyone make his father and his embarrassing behaviour disappear.

On some level since then, he'd wanted to have that control, and as he'd grown older, he'd wanted to *own* that control. Ironically he'd never felt in less control right now.

Instead he just said to Aneesa, 'I went to college and studied business and economics. Once I inherited my share of my father's money, I invested it in a hotel in London which was just a shell of a dilapidated Georgian building. It's right beside an old church, so I saw the potential for it becoming a wedding venue as well as being a perfect base for a hotel. I had an excellent architectural design team, and once that one had taken off, the rest followed all around the world.'

'You must have been so young—that's an incredible achievement.'

He looked at Aneesa and was blinded momentarily by the chocolate brown of her huge eyes, and the way she was backlit by the inky starry London sky. He cursed himself. What was wrong with him? He hated the pride that suffused him even as he clamped down on it.

The truth was, that for all of his success he'd long ago dismissed compliments as they invariably came with strings attached. But Aneesa had sounded utterly genuine. He came from a family of high achievers and had never felt that his had been any more than anyone else.

He looked away. 'I was young, yes, but no younger than you when you became a success.'

Aneesa felt the sting of his tone. He hated talking about himself and his innate modesty made something inside her feel weak, when she was used to dealing with huge egos.

'You have a lot of brothers and…one sister?'

He glanced at her and again she had the distinct impression that he was only answering on sufferance and at any moment he'd clam up and tell her to mind her own business.

'I have five half-brothers and one full brother, Nathaniel, the actor.' Something indecipherable flashed in his eyes before he said, 'And yes, I've one sister, Annabelle. She's a photographer.'

'Do you see them much?'

He looked at her properly now with a clear warning in his eyes and answered tightly, 'We're all in different places and see less of one another now, but if we're in the same city we endeavour to try and meet up.'

'Your father…?'

At that Sebastian rose to his feet with a fluid move. Tension crackling off his form. 'If you don't mind I have a couple of things to attend to in my study. I'll say goodnight.'

Aneesa nodded faintly and said goodnight, watching as he strode out of the room. *And I'll ask you not to poke your nose into my private life again* was all he hadn't said.

Aneesa put down her cup of tea and curled back into the chair. Sebastian was more of an enigma than ever. The fact that she was carrying his child clearly didn't give her access into his family history. And why was he so guarded about it? All she'd been able to glean from the tiny bit of research she'd done was that there had been some scandal, and that his father was dead…

and no matter that he said he saw his siblings, evidently they weren't all *that* close.

Aneesa forced her mind away from the torrent of questions and waited until she knew Sebastian was likely to be well ensconced in his study before she went to bed.

A couple of nights later Aneesa couldn't sleep and sat watching the gloriously beautiful inky skyline of London from her bedroom window. The questions reverberating in her head were no less now than they had been. But Sebastian couldn't have made it clearer that she'd strayed too far off the path. They'd shared meals, but he'd skilfully diverted all questions away from himself and focused solely on her. He was as stubborn as a mule.

And through it all, making Aneesa go slightly crazy, was the ever-ratcheting sexual tension she felt, when she had no indication from Sebastian that he felt the same.

She caught looks every now and then but he'd look away and she'd feel like she'd imagined them. That she was fantasising. And, she assured herself now, she *was*. Sebastian was putting up with her, that was all. They'd had one night, and that was it. The only reason they were together now was because of the consequences of that night.

She sighed deeply and had to acknowledge that, despite everything, she'd settled into Sebastian's somewhat ascetic apartment. She'd noticed his patterns of sleeplessness over the weekend, hearing him get up and move around or go out only to return an hour later, because invariably she was awake too, her body too hot to sleep. Hot with the changes due to the pregnancy and hot because she couldn't seem to stop having lurid X-rated dreams about him.

And she'd also noticed his punishing regime of exercising. If he wasn't out jogging he was down in the private gym either swimming length after length or punching a boxing bag.

She remembered that he'd been in the pool that night she'd burst into his suite in Mumbai. She longed to ask him why he insisted on such a regime but knew he wouldn't welcome her curiosity.

Despite mentioning his extensive family, he had no pictures of them dotted around the apartment. Aneesa thought nostalgically of her own chaotic family home in Mumbai where you couldn't move for knocking down a slew of pictures of her huge extended family.

If it hadn't been for Daniel, who lived in the apartment directly below Sebastian's, she would have felt very lonely. Aneesa had shown Sebastian her book on pregnancy and asked him if he wanted to read it, and when she'd seen the way he'd paled she'd hurriedly taken it back. She knew the baby hadn't been planned and that this was hardly a conventional situation but he seemed to react in such a viscerally negative way that she longed to know more about *why* that was. Even though she knew he was hardly likely to tell her.

Daniel had long gone home and Aneesa was in bed as Sebastian sat in a chair in his study and looked out at the glittering view of night-time London, with its millions of lives and stories unfolding.

The past few days had been torture for him. The reality of having Aneesa in his apartment—asking

questions, under his feet, around every corner, her
scent lingering in the air, listening to her husky laugh
while talking to Daniel—was enough for him to think
he was going demented. Her barrage of questions the
other night had made him feel like a cornered animal.
She'd pushed so many buttons at once that it had taken
all his restraint just to get up and leave her.

And yet, curiously, he felt no compunction to see
the back of her, which was a contradiction that did not
sit well with him. As if by osmosis things had already
started to appear—a bunch of flowers in a vase in the
hall which Daniel had defensively declared had been
for Aneesa, to brighten the place up; a cashmere scarf
thrown casually over the couch in the living area; a pair
of sneakers by the main door that looked tiny enough
to belong to a child which had precipitated the memory
of *that* night, when he had removed her wedding shoes
and kissed her hennaed feet…and there was still her
scent, everywhere her scent.

The thought of taking another lover while she was
here now was…impossible. As impossible as it probably would have been even without her presence. She
filled his every waking and sleepless moment. She was
all he saw when he swam length after length, or as
sweat dripped into his eyes when he punched out all
of his nameless aggression; and curiously for the first
time the aggression was harder to pull up. He found the
punch bag annoyingly ineffectual now. And he'd craved
it all weekend.

And the baby—all the talk of doctors and arrangements about this tiny being who was still being formed
had made him feel disconnected. Whenever Sebastian
tried to think about it, he felt a leaden weight inside

him, like he just couldn't connect with the reality. He envied Aneesa's clear bond; he saw the way her hand would unconsciously go to her belly and her face would soften, her eyes glowing with some secret light.

But the truth was, becoming a father terrified the living daylights out of him. There was so much to fear; that he would become as cruel and mercurial as his father had been. As irrational as it was, he had a visceral feeling that perhaps this could be passed down in the genes. And, how could he know that once Aneesa had the baby she wouldn't succumb to depression like his own mother had? It had been exacerbated to the point that eventually his mother had ended up in fulltime care when he and his brother had still been tiny. The effect of that had been devastating, and was still felt today.

He didn't want to be responsible for creating an awful legacy like his parents had, and had nothing to go on in terms of seeing how his siblings might handle it, as none of them had had children yet.

Sebastian had known very few moments of stability in his life, so to try and contemplate it now was… impossible. And in truth he didn't want to contemplate it because the memories it brought up were too painful. He'd already begun having *those* dreams again and knew it was the prospect of the baby that had sparked them…because he was terrified that any child of his would endure what he had endured.

But eclipsing all that was the raging burning desire for Aneesa. Every bone in his body ached for her—for her touch, her scent. To have her surround him like she had that night, with such sweet openness, such innate sensuality. He sought it now on an instinctive level almost as if he knew that she might have the power to calm the demons in his head. Even while she was the cause of some of them.

He'd told himself she was danger with a capital *D*, and that, she undoubtedly was. He'd had to struggle to maintain control of his animal impulses around her, and to rebuff her natural gregariousness and desire to know everything about everything, and everything about *him*.

At that moment, something inside him broke, some control he'd been clinging onto. She was here, in his life, pregnant with his child, and she wasn't going anywhere for the foreseeable future, and he needed release because he would explode if he tried to keep this wall up any longer....

With a rising sense of urgency and resolve firing his blood he stood and went straight to Aneesa's room. When he opened the door he saw that the bed was empty and immediately felt an uncomfortable lurch in his chest, but then he registered a movement near the window and saw her there, sitting on the wide window seat, legs tucked up under her chin, looking out at the view exactly as he had just been.

Except now she was looking at him and he could see those huge eyes widen. She wore a long T-shirt and her legs were bare and his body hardened in an instant. He walked over to her and she swung her legs down and stood.

'Sebastian? Was there something you wanted?' Her voice was husky and reached down inside him where he couldn't escape from this desire anymore.

He came right up to her and pulled her into his arms and already he could feel his mind settle, even as his heart thundered and his body ached. 'You, Aneesa…I want you.'

Aneesa barely had time to register what was happening before she felt Sebastian's mouth settle over hers and she groaned in supplication. He'd walked right out of her fantasy and into her room and for a second she'd thought she was dreaming. But it wasn't a dream when she could feel his tall lean length against hers, and his arms were wrapped around her so tight she could barely breathe. The sizzling, simmering tension she'd felt *hadn't* been one-sided—the relief made her feel faint.

With impatient hands he tugged at her T-shirt until she had to lift her arms and let him pull it off. He stood back for a moment, his eyes raking over her almost feverishly, and Aneesa felt a dart of trepidation at the heated fervour in his eyes, almost as if he'd consume her with just a look.

He started to take off his own clothes, practically ripping his shirt, yanking down his trousers, until he stood before her, naked. Not another word had been exchanged; they were both breathing heavily, desire saturating the air between them. The world could have stopped outside and they wouldn't have noticed, both greedily taking in the other's body as if relearning it.

With a shaking hand Aneesa reached out to touch Sebastian's chest before leaning forward to press a kiss against the hot silky skin. His hands tunnelled through her hair and caught her head, before he pulled her back up and looked down.

'You're so beautiful.' He shook his head as if in awe and something inside Aneesa was incredibly moved. His hands skated over her shoulders and moved down to cup her breasts which had grown bigger, and she sucked in a breath.

He stopped and asked, 'Are they sore?'

Aneesa tried to smile but felt too hot and desperate. 'They're a little oversensitive, but it's OK....'

With a touch so gentle it nearly made her cry, Sebastian cupped and felt the generous curves and then he bent his head and licked around one pebbled aureole before gently tugging the hard nipple into his mouth. The sensation was exquisite and on the knife edge of both pleasure and pain. Aneesa's head fell back, her hands holding Sebastian's head as he ministered lavishly to one breast and then the other.

And at that moment while the fire was raging inside her, she had a sudden memory of watching him leave the other night for his date, as well as all those pictures she had seen on the Internet of him with beautiful blonde women.

She pulled at his hair and yanked his head up. 'I won't sleep with you when you've been in another woman's bed so recently.'

Sebastian stood tall. His eyes glittered; his face was flushed, and he frowned. 'What are you talking about?'

Aneesa dropped her hands from his head and with every bone in her body protesting she bent down and picked up her T-shirt, slipping it on, back to front and inside out. She felt suddenly cold and wrapped her arms around herself.

'You were in another woman's bed the other night...' And then she blurted out because she couldn't stop herself, 'And I know you've got a reputation. So I won't sleep with you just because you're bored or to tide you over between lovers. Because clearly that's what happened in Mumbai that night.'

She looked down and then turned around when all she could see was Sebastian's gloriously naked and aroused body. She heard him drag his trousers on.

'Aneesa...'

She wouldn't turn around and she heard him sigh. She felt a hand on her shoulder turning her gently and then a finger under her chin tipping her face up. She averted her gaze stubbornly. He said, 'Boredom played no part in what happened that night, nor did it have anything to do with filling a convenient gap between lovers, nor does it now. Do you remember what I said to you? That I didn't normally do that?'

Aneesa half shrugged, still valiantly avoiding Sebastian's eye.

'It was the truth. I hadn't slept with anyone for weeks before that night. And then you came along and I've never felt desire so intense before.'

She still said nothing, wouldn't look at him. He sighed again.

'I didn't sleep with that woman the other night, and to be honest, even if you hadn't turned up on that day, I know I wouldn't have been able to sleep with her.' His mouth twisted. 'The only reason I arranged the date in the first place was because I couldn't get the memory of *you* out of my head. And then the only reason I kept the date was because it was a pathetic attempt on my part to deny how seeing you again made me feel.'

Aneesa's eyes darted to Sebastian now and she couldn't look away again. He held her chin firm.

'I haven't slept with anyone since that night in Mumbai.

And the thought of sleeping with any other woman apart from you quite frankly turns my stomach.'

Aneesa blurted out, 'Why didn't you want to see me again?' She stopped and faltered, hating the insecurity that prompted the question. 'I mean, it seems as if you have no problem taking lovers, so why didn't you want to contact me?'

Every self-protecting instinct within Sebastian locked into place and he gave her the only answer he could right now, knowing it was only the half of it.

'Because I knew you were different. You deserved more than I could offer. But now you're here…and I've wanted you every day since that night. I'm not strong enough to resist you…*this*.'

Aneesa looked into Sebastian's eyes and treacherously all of her fight drained away. She trusted that what he said was true, and while she suspected there was more to it, for now it was enough. Even though she had the leaden feeling that he was still warning her not to expect anything beyond transitory pleasures, baby or no baby. She needed him too badly. She'd hungered for him, and *ached* for him, and suspected that he'd just offered her more assurance than he'd probably given any woman. *And she carried his baby, his seed.*

She knew he was waiting for her move, so she reached down and pulled her T-shirt up and off again, dropping it to the floor. And stepping right up to him, she wound her arms around his neck and kissed him with all the pent-up fervour she'd been pushing down for weeks.

Within minutes they were naked and on the bed, limbs entangled, hot and sweaty, an urgency driving them both to seek that heady blissful union again. And it was only when Sebastian thrust deep inside Aneesa and her body welcomed him back with a glorious spontaneous wave of pleasure that she realised how deeply in danger she was of falling for this man.

If Aneesa had assumed that sleeping with Sebastian would mark a progression in their relationship, then she'd been very naïve. While for her it had precipitated the most cataclysmic realisation of her life—she was falling for him—for Sebastian it seemed to be fulfilling the sole purpose of sating a physical need.

For nearly two weeks now they'd been sleeping together every night, invariably in her bed. And without fail, Sebastian would get up and go back to his room. The one night when they'd ended up in his bed, he'd carried Aneesa, exhausted and sated, back to her own. When she'd protested he'd just bent down and pressed a searing kiss to her mouth and said, 'I'll only keep you awake…'

And if anything, Sebastian had become even cooler, more distant. It was as if their physical relationship was having a directly negative effect on any kind of emotional closeness. And yet, Aneesa knew instinctively that if she attempted to stop the physical side of things, Sebastian would retreat even more.

He was the father of her child and she knew it was dangerously idealistic but she couldn't help but dream of a future for them. And if she was ever going to reach him, and discover the secrets he kept hidden, then she would just have to bide her time. But right now, she bit back a feeling of futility as she headed to a doctor's appointment on her own.

When it came to anything to do with the baby,

Sebastian clammed up even more. He never asked her how she was feeling and, apart from discussing arrangements, showed no interest in his child, or her pregnancy. Even though when they made love she could tell he was aware of her small but growing bump.

He'd shown no interest in joining her at the doctor's today where she was due to have her first scan. When she came out of the appointment, the spring sunshine was strong. Relief was her predominant emotion—she was healthy and everything looked fine and normal with the baby.

She held the small printout of a picture of her baby in her bag, but she had no one to share the news with. People hurried past her on the street and a wave of loneliness and homesickness washed over her. She had a sudden feeling of empathy for all the Indian women who travelled to England each year to make a new life, quite usually with a new husband they might have not have even met before.

A moment of inspiration struck her and she called the apartment from a payphone to let Daniel know what she was doing, in case he worried when she didn't arrive home. And then feeling chirpier than she had in days, she joined the throng of humanity and disappeared into a nearby underground station, armed with a tube map and instructions from Daniel.

Sebastian stood at the window of his office, hands deep in his pockets. His insides roiled and he felt in turmoil. And whenever he felt like this, he retreated inwards. Which is what he'd been doing ever since he'd started sleeping with Aneesa again.

It had always worked for him in the past; at times of

stress or crisis, he'd retreat inwards and be at his most productive outwardly. Or he'd go off and do a triathlon and lose himself in the most gruelling physical thing he could think of. As a child it had manifested itself in taking out the horses his father had owned and riding until both he and the animal were shaking and sweating with fatigue, but exhilarated by the adrenalin rush. His mind would be numb from all pain, and the sense of isolation that had dogged him since his mother's exit from his life, and the fact that she'd shown an almost fatal preference for his younger brother Nathaniel, would leave him momentarily.

But now…the retreating inwards wasn't working the way it usually did. For a start, everything felt suspiciously close to the surface, as if there was a delicate shell around him that might crack at any moment. And even more worryingly, he didn't crave the opium of physical release the way he always had. Work held little interest for him. And the most disconcerting thing of all—he'd begun sleeping for long stretches, and waking at dawn, instead of arriving home at dawn, exhausted from a six-mile jog.

He consciously resisted the inevitable intimacy provoked by sex by retreating from Aneesa, maintaining a distance. And then guilt struck him hard. She'd gone to a doctor's appointment today—the first. He'd known about it, of course, and when she'd tentatively asked if he'd like to come, he'd issued a curt, 'No,' citing work. The thought of seeing that jumble of growing cells become a baby on a grainy black-and-white screen had made his innards seize with fear.

He grimaced now. The very work he'd cited hadn't held his attention because Aneesa was out there somewhere, and learning about her baby, *their* baby, without him. Galvanised into sudden action, Sebastian called the apartment and frowned when Daniel told him she wasn't home. He consulted his watch, a tendril of concern going through him. 'But the appointment should have been over an hour ago, plenty of time for her to get home.'

Daniel replied, 'She called to ask me how to get to Brick Lane—she said she'd read about it in a book—so I gave her directions....'

Sebastian didn't hear any more of what Daniel said. He remembered his security guard's awed reaction to seeing and meeting Aneesa that first day. She was one of Bollywood's biggest stars and she was headed to one of the busiest hubs of Anglo-Indian life in London.

Real fear curdled his insides as he slammed down the phone and bellowed to his PA to get his car brought around. With his heart hammering Sebastian cursed the fact that he hadn't even thought to get Aneesa an English mobile phone, and prayed that today of all days she was wearing a baseball hat and sunglasses.

Aneesa had got off the tube and was wandering along the main street of Bethnal Green, looking for Brick Lane, happily browsing through the stalls, soaking up the atmosphere and loving the colourful vibrancy of the area. She'd spotted a DVD shop that had a poster of one of her movies on the door. Even just hearing her native language being spoken made her smile. She congratulated herself on coming here when suddenly a passing woman caught her arm and exclaimed incredulously, *'Aneesa Adani?'*

Aneesa was startled for a moment. She'd almost

come to forget that people might recognise her. She switched on a smile and the woman was now shouting ecstatically to some friends to come over. Within seconds a small crowd had formed and Aneesa was being photographed with the group of women.

More and more people started to congregate as they noticed the fuss and saw who it was. They couldn't believe that a real-life Bollywood star was in their midst. Aneesa was starting to get jostled as people tried to pass and the newcomers wanted photos and her autograph. It was only when she was nearly knocked over that she felt the first real spiking of fear and looked up to see nothing but a vast sea of faces around her.

The crush of the crowd registered then and belatedly she started to try and turn back, smiling apologetically. She'd never had to deal with anything like this before, as in Mumbai they'd always been surrounded by security teams. But now she was thousands of miles from Mumbai and surrounded by a growing crowd of complete strangers.

And then the mood started to change. An old woman pushed her way forward and spat at Aneesa's feet and issued an insult that made Aneesa blush. Evidently the news of Aneesa's pregnancy had spread to England from the tabloids in Mumbai.

And then another woman appeared and started to reach for Aneesa's head as if trying to pull her hair. Aneesa felt real panic set in, and fear that she and the baby might be harmed. She put a protective hand on her belly. She could see nothing but the crowd and knew that if she didn't escape soon she'd be sucked under completely. Even as she thought that, the crush got even more intense and people starting to fight one another, defending her and lambasting her in equal measure.

With a useless scream strangling her throat she tried to look around to seek escape and could only blink stupidly when she saw a car screech to a halt at the side of the road, and the tall grim-faced figure of Sebastian emerge from the back. He waded through the crowd with singular intent. When he got to her, he effortlessly plucked her up into his arms where she clung onto his neck and curled up as tight as she could into his chest. And it was only at that moment, as she could feel his strong body beneath hers, that she believed he was real and relief flooded her.

By the time they got to his car and were safely ensconced and driving away, she was still curled on his lap and trembling violently. Sebastian issued soothing words and stroked her back as if she were a child and finally she'd calmed enough to look up and stutter out, 'How…how did you know?'

He tilted his head back so he could look at her and brushed some of her hair behind one ear. 'Daniel told me.' His jaw clenched and it was only then that Aneesa registered the extreme tension in his body. 'And thank God you'd told him where you were going. I saw the crowd just before we got to Brick Lane.'

Aneesa shook her head. 'I didn't even make it there. I had no idea—I didn't think for a second something like that might happen.' She started to tremble again as she recalled the way the crowd had just materialised within minutes and crushed around her. And then that woman's face twisted with anger.

She shuddered. 'They were nice at first but then an old woman started saying the most vile things about me and my baby.' Tears threatened and Sebastian kissed her, placing his hand on her belly, touching her there for the first time with intent.

'They're a traditional community. Look at how you had to leave Mumbai. Anyone that threatens their traditions threatens them, and ex-pats will cling onto that world even more fiercely.'

Aneesa nodded her head, biting her lip, struggling to regain control, but his hand on her belly was making her feel even more raw. She felt like she was always weeping all over Sebastian. 'I know...but it was just a shock to see it up so close like that....'

And then Sebastian's hand tightened on her belly and he said gruffly, 'And it's my baby too. Our baby.'

Aneesa looked at him and also noticed for the first time how pale he was. He shook his head now. 'When I saw you in the middle of that mob...' He couldn't finish. 'I'm sorry for not coming to the doctor with you today. I shouldn't have let you go on your own. I won't let that happen again.'

More stupid tears threatened. 'It was fine, really...I don't mind. I know that it can't be easy for you to come to terms with this.'

He was grim. 'Nevertheless, I'm coming next time.'

Aneesa finally relaxed her death grip from around Sebastian's neck and he shifted slightly under her so that she fell into the cradle of his lap more. She blushed at the intimacy. She went to move off his lap but he pulled her back with a growl. 'Stay where you are. You're not going anywhere alone again without a team of bodyguards.' She felt him take a deep breath before saying, 'I know I've been avoiding lots of issues, especially around the baby, and I'm going to be there more from now on.'

Unable to halt the rising tide of tenderness because she could see something achingly vulnerable in his blue eyes, which she *knew* he would hate her to see, she just caressed his jaw and said softly, 'Thank you.'

And she pressed a kiss to his mouth, weakly succumbing when his tongue sought hers and stoked the fires of their relentless desire.

For the rest of the day Sebastian treated Aneesa like she was made of bone china, to the point where she had to curb her exasperation when he insisted on carrying her from the dining table to the bedroom after dinner. It had been bad enough dealing with Daniel's guilt-ridden hand-wringing all evening too. The man had been beside himself to know that he'd unwittingly let Aneesa walk into certain danger, and nothing she could say would make him feel better.

But now all of her impatience melted when Sebastian put her gently on her bed and asked her, 'Did you get a scan picture of the baby today at the doctors?'

Aneesa nodded and got up to fetch her bag, her heart thumping unevenly. There had been more than a hint of nerves in Sebastian's voice. She pulled out the scrap of paper with its distinctive black-and-white image and handed it to him, smiling wryly. 'It doesn't really look like much now.' She sat cross-legged on the bed beside him and pointed out the curved spine and the head. Then she put a hand on her belly and said wonderingly, 'I can't really believe that's inside me, especially when I can't feel anything moving yet....'

Sebastian was just looking at the paper, his face intent. Emboldened by this perceptible softening and the way he'd been so gentle and tender all evening she asked hesitantly now, 'I saw something in the papers about your brother Nathaniel's wedding in a few days at your hotel… Are you going?'

Immediately Sebastian tensed beside her and Aneesa was afraid he'd get up and walk out. His jaw went taut but he didn't move and finally said in a tight voice, 'No, I'm not going to the wedding. And I'm not interested in discussing it.'

Feeling scared but knowing it was important, she asked, 'What if I want to discuss it?'

Sebastian avoided her eye. 'Please, Aneesa, don't push me on this.'

Before she could ask any more questions or her far-too-perceptive eyes could see the effect that looking at the picture of his baby was having on him, Sebastian handed her back the printout, got up abruptly from the bed and muttered something about running a bath for her.

He escaped to the bathroom, feeling like an utter coward. But the truth was that his entire world felt like it had just tilted sideways. Her questions had cut far too close to the bone, especially now that he knew his brother Jacob was seemingly intent on getting everyone together. And the knowledge hit again; that grainy image he'd just held in his hand was his son or daughter… And for the first time it wasn't the dreaded fear that threatened to overwhelm him but something that felt suspiciously like joy.

To his relief, after she'd had her bath, Aneesa seemed content to drop the questions. Sebastian didn't attempt to make love to her, even though his body screamed for it. And even though he felt a disturbingly primal need to brand her in some way—the aftermath of the terror he'd felt earlier was still in his system—but he controlled his urge. She was lying on her side, tucked into his body, his arms wrapped around her. He felt raw, like a layer of skin had been ripped away. Her breaths were deep and even and he told himself he'd get up and leave in a minute, but he couldn't stop his eyes from closing and the elusive tentacles of sleep bind around him.

The only way Sebastian knew he'd been having that dream again was because he was struggling for breath and something or someone was holding him down. He fought to get free and lurched off the bed, only realising then where he was.

Aneesa was looking at him with huge eyes, her hair tousled around her shoulders. 'You were having a dream…crying out for someone to come to you.…'

On jelly legs Sebastian walked over to the window. His heart was still hammering and his skin felt clammy. He spoke because something within him couldn't remain silent. He'd bottled this up forever.

'I was calling for my mother.'

'Yes,' Aneesa said quietly.

He was still half conscious and recounted the dream almost without realising he was doing it. 'I'm in my home where I grew up, Wolfe Manor, and I'm tiny. I'm in a dark corridor all alone, and I know something terrible has happened. I'm frightened and crying but no one comes and then suddenly there are lots of people—my half-brothers and -sister, our housekeeper…my father. But they can't see me and they keep rushing past me, even though I'm crying.'

Sebastian knew Aneesa had moved to sit on the edge of the bed. Silently he begged her not to come near him or he might crumble completely.

'Sebastian it was just a dream…' Aneesa's heart went out to the tall proud man who stood with his back to her.

He turned around then and she was shocked at the bleak look on his face. 'That's it, you see. It's not just a dream. It's a memory. When I was just over a year old, my mother walked into the lake on our estate and tried to kill herself and my brother Nathaniel. He was just a baby at the time, but my father was enraged because she'd been stupid enough to have another child. It was only because two of my older brothers saw her and saved them that they survived.'

Aneesa sucked in a breath. 'That's horrific…'

He smiled but it was grim. 'Yes. And there's plenty more where that came from, like the fact that my oldest brother Jacob had a row with our father which resulted in his death.'

Aneesa tried to speak. 'Sebastian—'

He made a slashing gesture with his hand. 'No. I won't discuss this anymore. You need to get back to sleep. I'm sorry for disturbing you.'

And he strode out of the bedroom. Aneesa just sat there for a long moment before curling back into bed, hugging her arms around herself. She didn't want to be alone tonight—she still felt vulnerable after what had happened earlier—but she knew there was no way Sebastian would come back now. She'd just pushed him to his limit.

CHAPTER SIX

WHEN Aneesa woke the next morning and went to get some breakfast, she wasn't surprised to see that Sebastian had already gone to the office. Daniel passed on a message to say that Sebastian would be working late, so not to wait up. Aneesa sighed deeply. They'd gone about five steps forward and three hundred back. All night she'd had broken and disturbed dreams about a small boy standing distraught in a dark corridor while people rushed past, ignoring him.

Great, she thought to herself as she poured some tea, *now I'm even taking on his nightmares*. But there had been something so sadly poignant about the image… and even now she silently vowed to protect her own child from any similar scenario.

After breakfast she went into Sebastian's study which he told her she could use to make calls home or for the Internet. Feeling determined, she sat there for hours and trawled the Internet for every bit of information she could find about the Wolfe family. She managed to find out a lot more this time and it was only when Daniel knocked and called her for supper that she realised how engrossed she'd become.

Her head spun with information she'd found, but

she'd ended up with nearly more questions than answers. By all accounts, William Wolfe, Sebastian's father, had been a charismatic and upstanding man of society. A vastly wealthy and enigmatic character, he'd had seven children, and a rumoured illegitimate son, the famous Brazilian entrepreneur Rafael da Souza. He'd clearly been a lover of women, with three marriages and at least a couple of love affairs to his credit. And yet all of his relationships seemed to have ended in tragedy, or mysterious circumstances. And exactly as Sebastian had said, he'd died by the hand of his own eldest son, although this tragedy had been ruled accidental.

There'd been one mention of Carrie Hartington, Nathaniel and Sebastian's mother, to say that she'd been committed to psychiatric care twenty-five years before, and nothing about where she was now. Aneesa could only guess, after what Sebastian had revealed, that perhaps his mother had had some sort of severe postnatal depression, because surely her own husband couldn't have driven her to such a situation?

All in all, as she dropped exhausted into bed that evening, Aneesa knew that the real story of Sebastian's past lay between the lines of everything she'd read today, and she also knew that he would have to be the one to tell her. She woke up a couple of hours later when she felt Sebastian slide into the bed behind her, his naked body tucking around hers. On a wave of relief that he'd come to her, she silently turned to face him and took his face in her hands, kissing him on his mouth.

Her nightdress was discarded in a matter of seconds and Aneesa said nothing as she and Sebastian made love. Afterwards, when he tried to pull away to leave, she gripped his arms around her and said determinedly, '*No.* Stay till I fall asleep.'

She could sense his struggle but finally he gave in, and for the first time, Aneesa lay awake while Sebastian slept. She prayed he wouldn't have the dream again, and finally fell into a dreamless sleep herself.

When she woke the next morning alone in the bed, Aneesa had to wonder for a moment if she'd dreamt that Sebastian had come to her the previous night, but then her naked and pleasantly aching body told her the truth.

Without even getting out of bed, she instinctively knew that Sebastian would be gone to work already and a small fire of anger and determination lit in her blood. She was *not* going to let him treat her as if she existed purely to keep his bed warm, and not even as a human being he could communicate with. She was carrying his child—she deserved better than that, no matter what secrets his past held.

Sebastian felt disgruntled and irritated. Ever since the horrific realisation that Aneesa had witnessed his most vulnerable moment, when he'd blurted out his dream, he'd been determined to do his best to mark out his territory again. Reclaim his *sanity*.

He'd gone into the office yesterday and had instructed his assistant to find apartments for sale or rent. He was going to move Aneesa out, or he'd move out if he had to. She could have the apartment and Daniel. He couldn't stay there any longer. With her. With those huge eyes watching his every move, silently questioning him.

So last night he'd come home, with arms full of

brochures for houses, determined to lay them all out and offer them up to Aneesa. He would set her up in style, so that she and his baby would never have to want for anything. He'd do the same in Mumbai if she so wished so he could keep them at arm's length and get on with his life.

And he would be calling a halt to the physical side of their relationship; it wasn't fair to keep sleeping with her when he had no intention of making her a permanent fixture in his life. He couldn't shake his visceral deep-rooted fears and simply could not envisage a future as a happy family.

But then…he'd come into her room where she lay sleeping and a force greater than he could resist had made him shed his clothes and climb into bed with her. He'd *had* to touch her. And then she'd turned to him and kissed him so sweetly and he'd been lost…and worst of all, afterwards he'd *slept*, until dawn had been breaking outside. His main feeling on waking up had been relief that he'd not had the dream again and his arms and hands had been full of soft, curvaceous and warm woman. One hand had rested across her belly, as if even in sleep it had gone there to protect the child within.

That soft yet hard swell had made a light sweat break out on his brow, but even so, the prospect of sending her away from him in that moment had sent panic through his system. So once again, with his head thumping with a mass of contradictions, he'd left so that he could avoid seeing her wake, seeing those eyes widen and the inevitable questions form.

That morning Daniel had gone out to do some shopping and Aneesa had declined to join him, still a little nervous of going outside, even though Daniel had informed her that Sebastian had two bodyguards standing by. Somehow Aneesa had known that the only person she would feel safe with was Sebastian.

So when she was passing the study and she heard the phone ring, she went in to answer it, her heart tripping to think it might be him. But it wasn't. It was another voice which sounded eerily familiar, deep and authoritative. When he asked for Sebastian and she said he was at work, the man sighed deeply and then said, 'Is this Aneesa Adani?'

'Yes…' she replied warily. 'Who is this, please?'

A long silence and then, 'It's Jacob Wolfe, Sebastian's brother.'

'Oh.' Immediately Aneesa thought of the fact that this man had been responsible for his father's death.

'"Oh" is right,' came the wry response. 'Sebastian hasn't responded to Nathaniel's wedding invitation. Do you know that our brother is getting married this weekend?'

'Yes…' Aneesa said, her head buzzing with questions. 'I'd heard…read about it in the paper. But I don't think Sebastian intends to go.'

'Somehow I'm not surprised.' Another silence fell and then Jacob said, 'Speaking of the papers, I saw you with my brother.'

Aneesa frowned. 'What do you mean?' And then she went paler and paler as Jacob described how pictures of Sebastian carrying her to safety from the mob on Bethnal Green had been tabloid front-page news for the past couple of days. She closed her eyes; she could just imagine the lurid headlines.

'Do you mind me asking—is it true? Are you having a baby with my brother?'

Miserably Aneesa figured it wouldn't have taken long for the hacks to get that information from the Indian papers and answered, 'Yes.' She hadn't even told her parents who the father was yet.

'Well, then, you must come to the wedding, even if Sebastian won't. You're part of the family now, and everyone would love to meet you.'

Aneesa gripped the phone cord tighter. Here was a chance to get to know more about Sebastian's past. Jacob was right; she was part of this family now whether Sebastian liked it or not.

'OK…' she said huskily, 'I'd like that very much.'

Jacob became brisker. 'Good, we'll see you at the weekend, then, and tell Sebastian I called.'

It was only when Aneesa put down the phone that some instinct made her pull open the top drawer nearest to her on the desk, and inside she saw it—the invitation to Nathaniel's wedding, torn neatly in half. The fact that he hadn't destroyed it completely sent a flicker of hope through her. She picked the two halves out and, with a sense of determination, found some sticky tape and stuck them together again.

And then when she was on the way out of the study, her head still spinning, she spotted them. Sitting on the edge of the desk. A pile of glossy brochures, all detailing luxury one- and two-bedroom apartments for sale or rent just nearby Sebastian's apartment. And worse… luxury apartments in Mumbai.

Hurt lanced Aneesa so badly that she had to suck in a breath. And then she heard a door slam, long strides coming towards the study. The door was flung open and

Sebastian stood there, resplendent in a dark suit. Every inch the successful and powerful titan of industry.

He frowned. 'What's wrong?' And Aneesa knew she must look pale. She shook her head and bought time to recover.

'What are you doing home?' She cursed her tongue, *as if this was home*.

Carefully now Sebastian said, 'I forgot a document I need for a meeting.'

Aneesa held the patched-up wedding invitation high in one shaky hand and said, 'Was it this?'

And then with the other hand she held up the sheaf of glossy brochures. 'Or perhaps it was these?' She glanced at them, and back to Sebastian. 'I haven't had the chance to look through them properly yet but perhaps a penthouse apartment isn't the most practical place for me to live once the baby gets here.'

CHAPTER SEVEN

INARTICULATE rage boiled upwards within Sebastian. 'How dare you go through my personal things!'

Aneesa stood before him, pale and intensely vulnerable-looking but with an unmistakably determined glint in her eyes. Her chin came up. 'I dare because as your own brother just told me, I'm a part of your family now and will be for a long time to come, thanks to *our* baby.

'Tell me,' she asked conversationally, colour returning to her cheeks, 'was last night just a quickie before you asked me to move out, or were you planning on taking your fill before my body becomes too rounded and repulsive to you?'

'Stop it,' Sebastian said curtly, the thought of her body growing more rounded having the complete opposite effect on his body. And before she could say anything else he asked, 'What did you mean about my brother?'

Aneesa leaned back against the desk, still holding the wedding invitation and the brochures. 'Jacob just called. He wants to know why he hasn't been able to get in touch with you and if you're coming to Nathaniel's wedding.'

Acute pain lanced Sebastian to hear that name. 'I've already told you I'm not going and it's none of his business.' He put out an imperious hand. 'Give me the invitation.'

Aneesa held it to her chest. 'No. If you want it you can come and get it. And you could have got rid of it properly but you didn't, so what does that say?'

Sebastian strode towards her then, fury all over his face, but Aneesa didn't feel scared. He stopped a couple of feet away and she could see the agitation on his face, in his blue eyes. His hands were fists by his sides. Tension bounced off him in waves.

Aneesa stood strong. 'I'm not giving you the invitation because it's not yours anymore. It's mine. Jacob has asked me to go and I've said yes.'

Sebastian's jaw clenched. 'You can't go. You don't even know them.'

Aneesa glared up at him. 'I might not know them but apparently now that we've been splashed all over the papers, they want to get to know *me*. They, unlike you, seem to be coming to terms with the fact that I'm carrying a Wolfe heir a lot quicker than you!'

'He saw the papers...' It wasn't a question.

'Yes. Why didn't you tell me?'

Sebastian raked a hand through his hair, exasperation evident. 'I didn't want you to be upset by it.'

'Perhaps you didn't want me to get any notions of permanency? You're forgetting that I'm not the one with the issues surrounding this pregnancy, *you* are.'

She looked at the brochures she held in her hand again and then stalked to Sebastian, pushing them into his chest where he had to catch them or let them fall. 'And it's apparent now that you're going to do your damnedest to get rid of all the evidence—shut your inconvenient ex-one-night stand away with her even more inconvenient baby.'

She walked past him to the door and turned back. 'I won't go to a place of your choosing like some pregnant concubine, Sebastian. I'd prefer to take my chances and return to India rather than endure that. And whether you like it or not, I'm going to your brother's wedding. I want my child to know his or her family.'

Aneesa was shaking by the time she reached her bedroom. Trembling all over. Standing up to Sebastian's rigid stance had been a lot harder than she'd thought, and still that awful hurt lanced her, right through her belly, to think that he would want to shut her and the baby away like that. And yet what else had she expected? Despair gripped her.

She was sitting on the window seat and looking out at the view, not really seeing it, just waiting for the inevitable sound of the front door slamming as it heralded Sebastian's return to work and away from her. But it didn't come. And when a knock sounded on her door, her nerves were so tightly wound that she jumped.

She stood to see the door open and Sebastian standing there, his tie ripped off, jacket gone and shirt open. And he looked so damned gorgeous that every bone in her body wanted to melt. But she stood firm with arms crossed, fully prepared to tell him that she was going to return to India after the wedding if he was going to insist that she move out.

'Don't you have work or a meeting or something? I don't want to be accused of disrupting your routine.'

Sebastian closed the door behind him and smiled grimly, making Aneesa's heart thump unevenly. He rested against it and said without rancour, 'I've cancelled my meeting, and my routine got disrupted the moment I first saw you in Mumbai.'

Hurt gripped Aneesa again. 'Well, I'm sorry about that but—'

He put up a hand. 'I'm not.'

And then he prowled towards her and she wished she could run but the window was at her back. Sebastian being cold and distant and prickly was one thing, but this more ambiguous Sebastian threatened every level of her already shaky equilibrium.

He stood before her, close enough to touch but not touching, eyes raking her face. Resting on her mouth with indecent explicitness before climbing upwards again where their heat nearly made her wobble.

He growled out, 'You're a thorn in my side, Aneesa Adani, but a thorn I'm finding impossible to ignore, no matter how much I try.

'I admit that I had thought of offering you a place of your own to live, ostensibly to get out you out of my apartment…but every time I try and push you away I find myself pulling you in again. I can't have you near me and yet I can't stand the thought of you not being here.…'

Aneesa's heart thumped crazily now. 'That sounds messy.'

Sebastian grimaced. 'It is. Very. Especially when my life up to now has been very clear and controlled.'

His eyes held her mesmerised. 'I told you that I would take more time out for you and the baby and then I promptly went back on my word. I'm sorry.'

He came closer then and Aneesa found it hard to breathe, her gaze slipping to his mouth. His hands went to her waist, pulling her into him, and she could feel his arousal, her own body rejoicing helplessly, despite all the turmoil in her head.

Valiantly though, she stayed rigid in his arms. She put her hands on his chest and tried to ignore the treacherous melting in her groin. 'Sebastian, you can't keep doing this, pulling me in, only to push me away again. It's not fair.'

'I know,' he said quietly. 'I don't think I have the strength to push you away again.'

He sighed heavily and she felt his chest move against her hands. A slither of foreboding went down her spine. 'But, Aneesa, I also can't promise you a happy ever after. There are dark secrets in my family, bad things happened. It's a long legacy of hurt and pain. And the last thing I want to do is visit that on my own child.'

Everything in her rejected that assertion. 'But you wouldn't—'

Sebastian put a finger over her mouth, stopping her words. 'After everything I witnessed, I won't commit just for the sake of propriety. My father wreaked havoc with his inconsistency and I can't promise to be any better.'

An aching sadness welled inside Aneesa even though she appreciated his candour. He was basically saying his feelings for her weren't strong enough to risk overcoming his fears. And was she strong enough to weather his stubbornness? To try and make him see that history didn't have to repeat itself? What was the point if he didn't even have feelings for her beyond physical desire?

And then as if he'd heard her thoughts, he said heavily, 'If you want to return home, then I won't stop you, and of course I'll come to visit when the baby is due. But if you decide to stay in England, here with me…you have to know that I can't promise anything more than I've already given.'

Aneesa quelled the urge to cry at Sebastian's searing honesty. He was offering her a no-win situation and only an extreme masochist would take the option she was about to. 'I can't go home yet, especially if the news has broken there as to who the father is. I should call my parents.' Her eyes lifted from where they'd rested on a button on his shirt. 'So I'm afraid you're stuck with me for now.'

'Are you sure about this, Aneesa?'

She nodded her head because, at that moment, she wasn't sure at all but she knew that the thought of walking away from him was far harder to contemplate than the alternative.

'Well, then, after you've called your parents we've got shopping to do.'

She frowned. 'Shopping?'

Sebastian's jaw clenched. 'If you're determined to go to this wedding, then you're not going on your own.'

Aneesa held in a stunned gasp and damped down a spark of hope. Sebastian was saying one thing, but his actions were saying something else, and despite her head sending out warning bells, her heart couldn't help but give a little lurch of treacherous hope. Grimly she answered, 'I'm determined.'

Sebastian sighed. 'In that case, I need to get a suit and you need to get a wedding outfit.'

Aneesa was not like any woman Sebastian had ever known. She was brave: brave enough to deal with the collapse of a successful career, to deal with ostracism and cross the other side of the world to face up to a huge personal crisis. And yet her eyes had filled with tears only that afternoon when they'd witnessed a harried mother clipping her small son around the ear on the street with enough violence to make him squeal with genuine pain. Afterwards Aneesa had apologised to Sebastian and said, 'I'm sorry—it must be my hormones.'

But it had made Sebastian feel even more strongly about his reasons not to commit. When he'd seen the child being brutalised on the street, he'd just felt sympathy for him, but not shock. And it was that sense of being anaesthetised that scared him.

He'd grown up learning to duck from his father's loose fists. He'd invariably been protected by one of his brothers and witnessed them getting a dose of physical violence, but none more so shocking than his beautiful older sister, Annabelle, the day their father had whipped her mercilessly, leaving her with permanent scars. He'd been too small to step in and help her and that sense of ineffectualness had stuck with him, heightening his sense of isolation. And his sense of fear that perhaps he couldn't protect his own child.

When they'd bought his suit for the wedding, he'd led Aneesa to a well-known designer shop on Bond Street, but on the threshold she'd pulled back and he'd looked down to see her face, puce with embarrassment. He'd frowned. He would have thought she'd have been running in, eager to indulge. But when she'd refused to budge she'd finally admitted, 'I don't have enough money to pay for a dress here. Let's go somewhere else. *Please.*'

And gruffly, he'd assured her that he'd intended to pay for her outfit, but still, she hadn't budged until he'd promised to let her pay him back.

She'd been quick and economical, settling on a knee-length champagne-coloured dress that had swirled around her like a diaphanous cloud, with a clever empire line to disguise her swelling belly. And a short gold blazer jacket to go over it.

When he'd seen her emerge from the changing room and how much delectable silky olive-skinned cleavage was revealed in the dress, he'd had to bite back the urge to insist on a less revealing dress. But she'd looked so shyly pleased that he hadn't had the heart to say anything.

It was only when they'd been headed back to the apartment that he'd realised how much he'd genuinely enjoyed the afternoon when he normally abhorred shopping, and how little he'd been thinking of the up-coming wedding. Especially when he'd made a vow not to see his brother Jacob ever again. But right now, with Aneesa by his side, the prospect wasn't half as daunting as he would have imagined.

On the morning of Nathaniel's wedding, Aneesa woke up and rolled over in the bed. Lying on her back, looking at the ceiling, she didn't need to feel the bed beside her to know that Sebastian hadn't joined her last night.

He'd been out indulging in his punishing exercise regime again, swimming or punching a bag, or running—she didn't know which. His rising tension as they'd approached the wedding had had a direct effect on Aneesa, to the point where his pacing in the living room last night had irritated her so much that she'd announced that his hair was too long and had made him sit down in the bathroom so she could give him a haircut.

He'd sat as meekly as a child while she'd moved around him, cutting his hair short, the way it had been when she'd first met him. When she was almost finished, he'd asked her gruffly, 'Where did you learn to do this?'

'My mother always cuts my father's hair. She taught me years ago.'

Their eyes had met in the bathroom mirror and she'd said drily but with a pain in her heart, 'It's just a haircut, Sebastian, don't worry. I'm not binding you to me for ever with some mystical Indian ceremony.'

But the truth was, she *had* found it more than a little erotic and all too easy to indulge in a fantasy of things being different. She'd never known what an intimate thing it was to cut someone's hair; perhaps it was because the other person was somewhat vulnerable. She'd always felt a little like a voyeur when she'd watched her mother tend to her father like that.

But afterwards Sebastian had got up and said an abrupt thanks and had all but run out, leaving Aneesa standing there holding the scissors, surrounded by hair. She'd felt like calling after him for a tip.

What she didn't know was that Sebastian had gone straight to his study where he'd poured himself a generous measure of whisky and downed it in one gulp. His hands hadn't been steady, the experience of having his hair cut by her affecting him more profoundly than he liked to admit.

Handing himself over to Aneesa like that—having

her caress his head, push it forward, tilt it back and to the side...running her fingers through his hair to judge where to cut, massaging his scalp...feeling the tantalising brush of her breast against his body—it had been all he could do to just sit there and not yank her round to sit on his lap and sate the fire burning in his loins.

Since when was getting a haircut erotic? And yet at the same time deliciously soporific? For the first time in a couple of days, since he'd decided to go to the wedding, she'd once again managed to distract him and shut out the clamour in his head...and he hated the feeling of vulnerability that gave him. The sense that, on some level, he *needed* her.

The elusive lure of losing himself in hard-core exercise had come to his rescue for the first time in days and he'd escaped to the pool where he'd swum himself to a point of exhaustion, finally falling asleep on a lounger by the pool as dawn broke outside.

Sebastian had told Aneesa that they would stay at his hotel the night of the wedding, so she'd prepared a small overnight bag, and when she emerged to the main reception area of the apartment there were butterflies in her belly to see the back of the tall, impossibly broad-shouldered figure of Sebastian in a steel-grey morning suit.

He'd been talking to Nathaniel on the phone and had agreed to be his groomsman. Apparently Nathaniel hadn't wanted a best man, and they were eschewing the traditional pomp and speeches for an informal late lunch after the ceremony. Sebastian turned around slowly now, increasing the butterflies in Aneesa's belly, and then she wondered if she was feeling the baby move for the first time?

But when his eyes hungrily took her in she forgot everything under his intense gaze. He'd seen the dress in the shop already, surely he liked it? She suddenly felt very insecure.

'Is it OK? It's not too short?' She pulled ineffectually at the dress and jacket.

'No,' Sebastian said curtly. 'It's fine.'

It was more than fine; she was quite simply the most beautiful thing he'd ever seen. A vision in gold and soft champagne. Her skin was glowing. Her long black hair was down and she'd teased it into sleek movie-star waves. And her feet were encased in vertiginous gold sandals that drew the eye to her slender but stupendously shapely legs.

He frowned. 'Can you walk in those?'

She stuck one leg out and he had to bite back a groan. 'I'll be fine,' she said breezily. 'One thing the movies and being a beauty queen has taught me is how to stand around for hours in high heels.'

He held out a hand. 'We'd better get going—' he smiled grimly '—wouldn't want to be late, now, would we?'

She came forward with a determined glint in her eye and took his hand, making his chest lurch. 'No, we wouldn't.'

The marriage ceremony was taking place in the small Unitarian church just beside the Grand Wolfe Hotel, which was huge and impressive—exuding a classic timelessness that Aneesa could recognise was Sebastian's trademark signature style.

Aneesa stood on her own for much of the service
as Sebastian stood alongside his brother. She recognised famous Hollywood actor Nathaniel, of course;
his hair was dark like Sebastian's but longer. When he'd
turned to greet Sebastian the two men had just looked
at each other for a long intense moment before hugging
fiercely. And with awful predictability emotional tears
had pricked Aneesa's eyes.

Nathaniel's bride, Katie, was stunning in a beautiful long ivory gown with antique diamante details just
below her bust and at the shoulders of the straps of the
dress, showing off her slender willowy frame. A mass
of brown curls was drawn up and away from her face,
highlighting a long neck and the most amazing green
eyes Aneesa had ever seen.

Aneesa had spotted who she assumed to be
Sebastian's other brothers ahead of her by a few pews.
They all cut tall intimidating figures. One she guessed
had to be Jacob, as he looked the most austere. She'd
caught a glimpse of his dark eyes when he'd turned to
watch the bride walk down the aisle, and they'd been
intense.

In the flurry of activity once the ceremony was over,
Aneesa was surprised when Sebastian reached for her
hand and pulled her from the pew so that she could
walk with him up the aisle. She felt the fierceness of his
grip and squeezed his hand silently, telling him that she
understood, touched by his obvious desire to have her
by his side. Once again that dangerous tendril of hope
unfurled inside her and she had to dampen it down.

There were paparazzi everywhere outside, like a
baying mob, being held back by a cordon of security
men. But Sebastian had them whisked inside the hotel

in minutes, and after checking with his manager that everything was running smoothly, they made their way to the main reception room.

Sebastian first introduced Aneesa to his sister, Annabelle, who Aneesa realised had been the photographer in the church and outside. She was beautiful—tall and slim, dressed with impeccably smart taste, with long wavy blond hair and grey eyes which swirled with emotion. Instinctively Aneesa guessed Annabelle wouldn't want people to see that and felt a small bond form between them, and was touched when Annabelle congratulated them on the pregnancy.

And then in no particular order she was introduced to the happy couple, who only had eyes for each other, and two other brothers, Lucas and Rafael, who'd been polite and inquisitive. Lucas's girlfriend, Grace, had been there also, tall with blond hair. Rafael, however, had shown that sparky Wolfe trait she was coming to know so well when Sebastian had asked after his wife, Leila. Rafael's black eyes had flashed warningly as he'd issued a curtly succinct, 'She couldn't make it.'

An enigmatic look had passed between Sebastian and Lucas.

Through it all Sebastian had his arm clamped around Aneesa's waist and her face was starting to hurt from smiling so much. And then she felt him tense rigidly. She followed his gaze to see a man approach them, the man she'd guessed was Jacob in the church. Tall with thick black hair, dark eyes like Rafael. And a grimly determined look on his face. Aneesa could feel Sebastian's urge to turn and walk away and she silently willed him to stay. He did.

But as the two tall men squared up to each other the

lengthening silence became unbearable. Aneesa might have been invisible for all the attention either man gave her, and then abruptly Sebastian issued a tortured sounding, 'I can't do this.' And letting Aneesa go, he strode away and out of the reception room.

Jacob's black eyes followed his brother and Aneesa could see the sorrow in them. She tentatively touched his sleeve and he looked down at her, finally focusing on her. Apologising, he introduced himself. 'I knew it wouldn't be easy for Sebastian after all this time, but I'd hoped…'

Aneesa felt awkward. 'I don't know exactly what happened between you but I'm sure it'll work out.'

Jacob smiled but it didn't reach his eyes. 'I hope so, but the truth is that I was the one person who Sebastian turned to after his mother was sent away, and after our father died, he was always the intensely quiet foil to Nathaniel's extrovert showmanship. They each found their own way of coping after their mother had to be committed…' He trailed off and then said, 'After I left…I knew that he might take it the hardest. But I had no choice.'

For a second Aneesa thought she had a flash of insight into Sebastian's psyche when she sensed that Jacob had felt unable to contain his own rage and emotions, and had left for that reason, to protect his own family. Did Sebastian share that fear? 'I'm sure you had your reasons…' Aneesa stopped then, feeling utterly useless. Sebastian hadn't been exaggerating when he'd warned her of their dark past. 'I…I should really go to him.'

Jacob caught her arm lightly as she turned to go. She looked back.

'I'm glad he has you, Aneesa.'

She just smiled but it felt brittle. She didn't think it the best time to get into the dynamics of her non-relationship with Sebastian. It looked like his brothers and sister had enough on their hands. But never more than now did she feel a sense of futility wash over her.

She went to the reception desk and got the key to their room, where their luggage had already been deposited. As the private lift whisked Aneesa silently upwards, she smiled politely at the slightly awed elevator attendant, who showed her to the door of the suite and opened it for her.

She slipped inside, heart thumping painfully. She walked through the rooms until she saw him, standing with his back to her, one arm above his head resting on the window which looked out over London's skyline. The other hand in his pocket, and his whole frame so rigid, her heart ached.

He didn't turn around. 'Not now, Aneesa, please. Just...leave me alone.'

The raw pain in his voice meant she had no choice. And she knew in that moment with a fatal inevitability that she loved him. She walked over to him and wrapped her arms around his waist, resting her cheek against his back, pressing close against him.

At first he stiffened and he brought his hand out of his pocket to cover hers as if to take her hands away, but then she felt a shudder run through his powerful frame and instead of extricating himself he laced his fingers tightly through hers and held her hands in place.

She could have wept for him and her throat ached at the turmoil she felt in his body. She knew he was crying but she guessed it wasn't with tears, she imagined it was like a kind of deep ache that went beyond tears, welling up from inside him. She could feel it like a physical sensation resonating within her. She didn't know how long they stood there like that with her arms tight around him, her body pressed against his, her bump pressing solidly into his buttocks, but at some stage Sebastian started talking, in such a low voice that Aneesa had to strain to hear.

He told her everything—about how utterly mesmerising his mother had been, but too fragile to be a real mother, and then how she'd disappeared into full-time care, which had been terrifying to a six-year-old. The constant crying and fighting between his parents before his mother had disappeared, and about his violent father and the highs and lows of his mercurial moods. How he would drunkenly wake them all up and initiate a magical ghost hunt in the woods surrounding the house on a midsummer night's eve which would then morph into a nightmare of gigantic proportions because one of the boys would have innocently provoked him into an uncontrollable rage.

He spoke about the fierce solidarity between his siblings who'd always looked out for one another, despite the fact that they weren't all full siblings. And about how, despite that solidarity, *he'd* never really felt a part of it, somehow always on the fringes, observing the action. He told her dispassionately about how his father had brutally whipped his sister, and about Jacob being the one constant who had never let him get too insular…until the day he'd left for good.

The setting evening sun was streaking the sky outside with dusky pink ribbons when Sebastian finally turned around in Aneesa's arms. He looked down at her and she stifled a breath. He looked haggard, his eyes bruised.

'Why are you here? Why are you listening to this?'

She gave a small shrug, her eyes never leaving his. 'Because you needed to tell someone. Because you're the father of my child, and because…' Her heart tripped for a second. She was half terrified she'd reveal just how much she cared about him. 'Because you were there for me when I needed someone…'

He quirked a small smile and relief flooded her belly.

'Yes, but instead of providing silent counsel and sending you on your way I threw you onto the nearest bed and made love to you within an inch of our lives.'

Aneesa took his hand from around her waist and pressed a kiss to his palm before saying, 'And I'm glad you did.'

He shook his head then, his face sobering up. 'I can't go back down there. I can't see him. I wanted to kill him. I've never felt such rage before.'

No, thought Aneesa, *because you've channelled it into physical things like burning your body out.*

He extricated himself from Aneesa's arms and walked over to the drinks cabinet where he poured himself a drink. Gently Aneesa pointed out, 'It's not just Jacob who is down there, it's Nathaniel and his new wife. And your other brothers, and sister. They all looked so happy to see you.'

He threw back the drink. She saw his fingers clench so tightly around the glass his knuckles shone white. 'Yes, but it's *him*. I won't give him the absolution he obviously wants, it's too late. He can't just arrive back into our lives like this.'

Aneesa walked over and turned him around to face her. 'So what? You're just going to avoid seeing him ever again? That's not exactly the adult response, is it?'

Before he could launch into an attack she said with soft determination, 'I know he hurt you, and badly, but no one is perfect, least of all us. Look at the car wreckage my life has been for the past few months. I've caused untold shame and misery to my family but despite that they still love me, and I know how lucky I am to have that. For a long time I was seduced by a much more shallow world, and I wasn't a particularly nice person. I took my family completely for granted, and yet when things fell apart they were still there for me.'

She pressed on. 'What you and your family went through was horrific, no one could dispute that, and from what you've told me, frankly I'm surprised that Jacob didn't leave a lot sooner. He obviously felt a huge sense of responsibility to you all.'

Sebastian issued a curt laugh. 'So huge that he left his vulnerable teenage sister still nursing the wounds of her attack from our father, and his younger brothers to the mercy of boarding schools and housekeepers for care?'

Aneesa said wryly, 'You turned out OK for all that second-rate care.' Then she bit her lip. 'Look, all I know is that my family had more than enough grounds to throw me out on the street and disown me after what I did to them. But they didn't. It's so much easier to see things in black and white and it sounds to me as if that's what your father did a lot of the time, fuelled by his drinking and rage.

'Can you not try and see things from Jacob's point of view?' Aneesa asked. 'Maybe he was scared he would become like your father, and cause more pain and harm? Perhaps he felt that that was his only option—to leave you all behind. Who knows what the guilt of killing a parent would do to someone even if it had been accidental?'

Sebastian felt as if Aneesa was flaying him alive with her words. She was coming far too close to his own inarticulate fears that he, too, might have carried his father's twisted moods and personality. The rage he'd felt just now when faced with Jacob had scared him with its intensity. He lashed out, sneering, 'You didn't mention the psychology degree you did in your spare time between Bollywood blockbusters.'

And the instant the words were out he wanted to swallow them back. He saw Aneesa's face pale and her chin come up. She said with the utmost dignity, 'I'm going to ignore that comment and give you the benefit of the doubt. And I'm going to go back downstairs to join your family and get to know them a little more. If you feel like you can stop wallowing in your childhood hurt and join the present, then you'll know where to find me.'

And on stiff legs she walked out, the door shutting with incongruous quiet behind her.

CHAPTER EIGHT

ANEESA was sitting beside Annabelle at one of the round tables where they'd just finished coffees. She didn't need to look around to know that Sebastian hadn't reappeared. She was trying to concentrate on the conversation but was still smarting from his cruel words.

She was also reeling with the knowledge that this beautiful, immaculately turned-out woman had been so horrifically beaten. Annabelle was being very sweet and explaining that her twin brother, Alex, was a racing car driver based in Australia, and couldn't be there.

Aneesa put a hand to her bump, only realising what she'd done when she noticed Annabelle follow the movement. She grimaced. 'It's still small, but it seems to be getting bigger by the day now.'

Annabelle smiled politely but then looked away with a small frown forming between her grey eyes. 'Jack should be here too, our elder brother, but I haven't seen him yet. I know Jacob wants to talk to him....'

Annabelle's eyes snagged and widened on something or someone else at the entrance to the room and Aneesa followed her look to see that Sebastian had returned and was in the doorway, with Jacob. Relief flooded her, and her silly heart swelled with love and pride. As she watched, Sebastian put out his hand but instead of shaking it, Jacob drew him into a fierce hug.

Her eyes smarting suspiciously now, and feeling dangerously emotional, she made a garbled excuse to Annabelle, saying she wanted to get something from the room. The waiters were starting to clear the tables and encourage people to get up so they could rear-range the room for dancing, so she wouldn't be missed. Instinctively she felt the need to give Sebastian some space with his family.

Once in the suite though, fatigue overcame her and she lay down for a while, unable to resist the lure of a nap when her eyes felt heavy. She woke up when she heard the door open and close and sat up groggily.

Sebastian appeared in the doorway, his jacket off and tie undone, looking rakishly handsome. 'Where did you get to?'

Aneesa sat up at the side of the bed and pushed her hair back. She felt at a disadvantage. 'I must have fallen asleep. I lay down just for a minute....'

Sebastian walked over and sat beside her; his distinctive scent made her stomach clench with desire. His eyes glittered an intense blue, all earlier signs of haggardness gone. He took a tendril of hair that had drifted down over her shoulder and let it slip through his fingers. He looked at her. 'I'm sorry for what I said earlier. I had no right to lash out at you, and you were too generous to give me the benefit of the doubt.'

'I saw you talking to Jacob.'

Sebastian smiled ruefully. 'You were right. We won't be fine overnight but I think we're going to be OK. Jacob is home for good. He wants to renovate Wolfe

Manor, restore it to its former glory, maybe even sell it. And I also found out that he was involved as a secret design consultant for this hotel, which was my first. So in his own way he has been watching over me from afar....'

Aneesa put a hand to Sebastian's jaw and felt the heady rasp of his stubble. Familiar heat coiled through her and she said huskily, 'I'm glad, Sebastian. I really hope it does work out for you all....'

Sebastian turned to face her fully, and with a slow intensity that made her toes curl he drew her close and kissed her, his arms trapping her against his chest. When he exerted a slight pressure so that she lay back down on the bed, she couldn't help the tiny moans of acquiescence and anticipation. He put his two hands on either side of her and pulled away, looking down at her. He ran the back of his hand down one hot cheek. 'If it wasn't for you I'd most likely be staring at the bottom of an empty whisky bottle now and cursing everyone and everything around me.'

She blushed and bit her lip. 'I did nothing except tell you what you already knew.'

His face came closer and he pressed a sweet kiss to her mouth. He drew back. 'It was more than nothing, and thank you.'

Suddenly breathless, she said, 'You're wel-come.'

'How welcome?' he growled with a dangerous gleam in his eye. Molten heat seeped through Aneesa's veins and she wondered a little desperately if she'd ever not want him so badly. She wrapped her arms around his neck and pulled him over her, relishing the friction of his chest against her breasts.

'*Very* welcome.'

Even as he kissed her and ran his hands down her body, Aneesa was conscious of a need to protect herself from the inevitable pain. And yet, when she felt Sebastian's hand travel up her bare leg under her dress, to find where she ached for him with such telling wetness, she couldn't concentrate on anything but his touch.

Pulling off her clothes first and then his own clothes with indecent haste, causing buttons to pop off his shirt and Aneesa to giggle, he came back over her and looked down into her eyes for a long moment. She was breathless, her naked breasts crushed against his chest, his body between her legs. And then without a word, he drew back and took her, with one cataclysmic thrust. So deeply that she could have sworn he touched her heart.

They didn't speak a word, but Sebastian's eyes never left hers, not even when she splintered around him with a small keening cry, her back arched. He just pulled one leg up, bending it back to that he could penetrate even deeper, and the next time she came within the space of minutes, just before he did. Aneesa couldn't stop helpless emotional tears trickling down her cheeks.

Sebastian just kissed them away, and turned them so that she was tucked into his chest with his arms tight around her, their hearts beating unevenly. But she couldn't stop the silent tears falling because she knew she was indulging in the fantasy that perhaps, just perhaps, this day and evening had marked a real change in their relationship. And she knew she'd be a fool to hope for that.

Aneesa woke at dawn to find herself alone in bed. Where Sebastian had lain close behind her was still warm, and guiltily she rolled back over and pressed her face into the pillow to breathe his distinctive scent deep.

Just then she heard a noise and looked up to see Sebastian emerge from the bathroom with a towel slung around his lean waist. She flushed guiltily and had a moment of déjà vu to when she'd woken after their night together in Mumbai.

'Morning.'

'Good morning.' Ridiculously she felt shy. Sebastian barely glanced at her and Aneesa felt it like a slap in the face, after the intimacies they'd shared last night. She had to repress an inexplicable shiver. She'd stupidly believed that possibly— She bit her lip and got out of the bed, drawing a hotel robe on, not that Sebastian was even looking at her. He was too preoccupied with something.

Even as she was thinking that, he dropped the towel with an ease that she thought she'd never get used to and started to get dressed, saying over his shoulder, 'I have some things to attend to this morning. My driver can drop you home whenever you're ready.'

Aneesa bit back the urge to ask him what exactly he could have to attend to on a Sunday morning. Last night and how intensely intimate it had felt trickled back into her awareness. Not to mention the emotional turmoil of the day. An awful suspicion settled into her belly like a cold weight. As it took root and grew, she said faintly, 'Don't be silly, you obviously need the car. I can take a taxi back to the apartment.'

Sebastian just shrugged and said, 'Whatever you want. I'll wait for you and we can leave together. I'll be downstairs. I need to check that everything went OK last night.'

Aneesa mumbled something incoherent and got through her shower in record time. Within a half an hour, hair still damp, she was downstairs wearing stretchy leggings and a tight-fitting long T-shirt under her leather jacket. Sebastian was pacing the lobby, looking like a beautiful caged panther, speaking on his mobile. When he saw her with her bag he cut the call short and ushered her out. Hailing her a cab he asked again if she was sure, and with her skin feeling clammy with panic she just said yes.

The awful familiarity of the pattern was all too obvious. Sebastian had opened up to her, shown her something of himself and now he was retreating behind those fortified brick walls again. She hated to find herself thinking like a suspicious lover but she *was*. He was so distracted he couldn't even look her in the eye.

He had to be seeking the habitual physical release he craved, except this time she had the awful premonition that it would be with a woman, and not through exercise. He must be hating the fact that she'd seen so much, that he'd been in any way vulnerable with her.

He barely waited till she was in the taxi before his own black tinted-window car was pulling away. Feeling ridiculous but compelled by a force greater than she could resist, she said to the driver, 'I know this is going to sound a bit silly but could you follow that car?'

The driver winked at her in the mirror and said in a broad cockney accent, 'I've been waiting forever for someone to ask me that!'

And with a none-too-discreet screech of tyres he executed an illegal U-turn and followed Sebastian's car.

They seemed to drive forever, and Aneesa saw signs for Surrey pass them by. Even the driver was getting concerned, asking her if she had any idea where he might be going.

Aneesa kept an eye on the metre and the money in her purse; as it was, she wouldn't have the return fare into town now and if Sebastian didn't stop soon— Just as she thought that, his car slowed and she begged the driver to keep back. The sleek black car stopped outside a pair of ornate gates and there was a discreet sign on the wall that said *The Grange*.

A house, a country house; it had to be. Where his mistress lived. Feeling nauseous, Aneesa instructed the driver to stop in a lay-by where she was just out of sight of Sebastian's car. She paid him and got out and watched him drive away. Feeling utterly ridiculous now, on wobbly legs she walked around the corner of the hedge fully prepared to meet a locked gate when she walked slap-bang into a solid wall of muscle.

Hard hands held her, blue eyes as cold as ice blistered down into her shocked ones. 'What the *hell* do you think you're playing at following me in that cab like some character in a bad movie?'

Too shocked to do anything but blurt out the truth, Aneesa just said, 'I thought you were going to meet a mistress or a lover so I followed you.'

Aneesa could see the play of emotions cross his face and even a glint of humour. She could deal with his anger better than pity. 'Don't laugh at me.'

Sebastian's face sobered and his hands became gentle on her arms. 'And what exactly were you planning on doing when you caught me with this mystery woman? Because presumably you were going to wait until we were *in flagrante…*?'

Aneesa shrugged but couldn't look away. The absurdity of it all hit her now too, and she said, 'Claw her eyes out?'

Sebastian just shook his head and said with a touch of weariness, 'Well, if you're so determined to meet this mistress of mine, then you'd better come with me.'

He took her bag, and Aneesa got into Sebastian's car and they swept through the gates and up a long drive. She was pretty sure there was no mistress now, but she had no idea what to expect, until they approached a huge stately home and she saw some people being pushed in wheelchairs by nurses in uniform.

They didn't stop there though; they kept going around the side of the house and down a nearby lane, shaded by the branches of huge oak trees. Finally they drew up outside a pretty cottage and a matronly woman opened the front door to greet them.

Sebastian came around to help her out of the car, and took her hand to lead her up to the path. The woman waiting for them spoke with a broad Irish accent. 'Sebastian! She's in good form today, looking forward to seeing you. She even got her hair done this morning.'

Aneesa followed Sebastian into a bright airy hallway and then into a sitting room where she saw a beautifully preserved woman looking out the window. She couldn't have been more than about mid-fifties, Aneesa guessed, and could have passed for even younger. The resemblance was striking even from her profile; it was clear where Sebastian got his patrician features from, and his blue eyes. *His mother.*

She turned as they came in, her whole face lighting up with joy. 'Nathaniel, darling!'

Sebastian squeezed Aneesa's hand as if to say, *Go along with it.* He let her go then to greet his mother. After a couple of minutes he pulled Aneesa around to introduce her, and to Aneesa's utter shock his mother took in her small bump which was revealed by the tight-fitting top and declared, 'You're pregnant! But how wonderful, my dear. Come and sit and tell me all about it. I do so love being pregnant too!'

Aneesa's head was reeling after a very bizarre conversation with Carrie where she'd constantly referred to Sebastian as Nathaniel, and seemed to believe she was pregnant as well. Eventually Sebastian said he'd take her out for a walk, and Aneesa took the hint and left them alone. The friendly Irish housekeeper came up to Aneesa and they watched Sebastian and his mother in the distance through the window.

The woman explained, 'I'm actually a psychiatric nurse, but she thinks I'm a housekeeper. I don't know how Sebastian does it, but every two weeks like clockwork he comes, and not once has she ever recognised him. He and his brother bought this old Gate Lodge for her so that she would feel as if it were her home. They thought it would be better for her than staying in the main psychiatric facility at the house. Also, here she's more protected, less chance of staff leaking stories to the press. She has full-time round-the-clock care....'

Aneesa asked hesitantly, 'Why does she think she's pregnant?'

The woman shrugged her shoulders and smiled sadly. 'We don't know for sure but it's obviously linked to when being pregnant was a happy time for her, so it's as if she's stuck there—in the past.'

After a few more minutes of polite conversation, the woman excused herself and Aneesa went outside. She told the driver where she was going, and started to wander back up to the main house, going in the opposite direction to the one Sebastian had taken with his mother. Her mind was buzzing, so many things falling into place.

It was time for Aneesa to face facts. It was glaringly obvious now where Sebastian's antipathy to becoming a parent stemmed from. He'd had no role model to speak of, and his brother, who had assumed both parental roles, had abandoned him at a vulnerable age. Her instinct that he would be a good father would hardly be enough to entice him to take on the role.

She and Sebastian might share an explosive chemistry, but clearly he resented it. Just as he resented the fact that she was seeing a side to him that he kept well hidden from everyone else. His cagey and secretive behaviour this morning was because he'd had no intention of telling her about his mother. But she, as usual, had lumbered in with two left feet and forced the issue into the open.

She recalled the tortured sound of his voice when he'd declared she was a thorn in his side. It was becoming very clear to Aneesa that the longer she stayed with him, the more resentful he would become. Eventually despising her for upsetting his life beyond recognition. For seeing more than he'd ever wanted anyone to see. She didn't doubt that his desire for her would wane once she was gone, and he could get on with his free and independent lifestyle.

The logical thing would be to take him up on his suggestion of moving into her own place, but she couldn't do that. London wasn't her home, and she couldn't bear to see Sebastian get on with his life right under her nose, checking up on her out of a sense of duty and because she happened to be having his baby.

This visit to his mother told her how deeply ingrained a sense of duty was to him and she didn't want to become his *duty*.

Aneesa was sitting on a bench in the sunshine when Sebastian found her a while later. She still felt a little numb inside at the decision she'd made. He sat down beside her. She looked at him and saw the lines around his mouth and could only imagine the untold pain of visiting a mother who didn't even recognise who you were.

'I'm sorry for assuming you were visiting a mistress, but I'm not sorry I met your mother.'

'She liked you.' He smiled wryly. 'Very possibly because she thinks you both have a lot in common, being pregnant.'

'Why does she think you're Nathaniel?'

His mouth tightened. 'Because he's the one she chose to take into the lake when she tried to kill herself. He's the one my father didn't want.' He looked at her and she shivered at the bleak look in his eyes. 'The fact that she recognised him as little as me over the years was no consolation. She was still obsessed by him. Do you know that for a long time I felt jealous of Nathaniel—because she'd chosen to try and kill herself with him instead of me?'

Aneesa couldn't stop herself from reaching out to touch Sebastian's hand briefly. 'I think that sounds entirely normal. And I think on some level she knows exactly who you are. You're doing a wonderful thing not to challenge her beliefs.'

They sat in silence for a few minutes and then Aneesa blurted out what she had to say, afraid that if she didn't say it now, she'd be too weak later.

'I need to go home, Sebastian. I want to be with my family.' She couldn't look at him, too afraid of the relief she might see on his face. The thorn in his side would finally be gone.

'I'm ready to go back, and be a mother on my own—I have no problem with that, but I will need my family around me. I was going to return sooner or later, it might as well be now.'

Sebastian turned and, compelled, she glanced at him. She couldn't read his enigmatic expression.

When Sebastian had woken that morning, and the previous day's and night's events had come back to him—along with the intensity of what he'd shared with Aneesa both physically and emotionally—he'd shut down. Curled away inside. He'd gone into his default self-protection mode. But Aneesa hadn't allowed him to hide away. She'd come along for the ride, *again*.

Her words impacted him now like a punch in the gut. She wanted to go home. Coming on the back of just being with his mother, who didn't even recognise him, he felt flayed inside, but recovered quickly. Why should he care either way that Aneesa wanted to go home? It had always been on the cards. He had to repress a cynical smile. Why wouldn't she want to run back to normalcy after witnessing the freak show that was the Wolfe family saga?

And yet…he knew plenty of women who would

happily deal with such skeletons and bask in the glory of unlimited wealth and status. Hadn't his own mother done that when she'd taken on William Wolfe and his brood of children? Aneesa was pregnant with his child. She had him over a barrel, yet clearly wanted nothing of his fortune, so by declaring she wanted to go home, nothing here was attractive enough to hold her. *Including him.*

She was proving once and for all that she was nothing like his mother and nothing like any other woman he'd ever encountered.

Her big eyes were looking at him now, making something inarticulate rise up within him. He smiled. 'Of course you want to go home.'

Her eyes narrowed. 'What's that supposed to mean?'

He looked away and shrugged, cursing himself for showing that it bothered him on any level. 'You always said you would want to go home.'

He could feel her penetrating look and tensed. She sighed. 'Yes, I did. And I think the time to go is before I turn into a total caricature of some kind of jealous lover.'

Her honesty surprised him. He was so used to women being vague, indirect.

Before he could dwell on the significance of that, she stood and said breezily, 'You made it very clear what would happen here. What you wanted. So I really don't see the point in prolonging my stay. Things should have died down at home, and I need to get prepared for the baby coming.

'That is—' her voice suddenly became more hesitant '—unless things have changed for you...?'

Sebastian looked up at her. The sun was behind her

and all he could see was her narrow framed silhouette. She had to be referring to the fact that he seemed to turn into a walking human emotional confessional around her. Was she asking him if he wanted her to stay because he might *need* her? Did she feel pity for him? Was she feeling a sense of responsibility to stay because he might have come to depend on her? Everything within him rejected that.

He stood, too, in an abrupt move and said curtly, 'No. Why would anything have changed?' He flipped out his mobile phone and called his car around.

When they were in the car, Aneesa tried not to let Sebastian see how she was trembling. It had cost her a lot to ask him if things had changed. She'd held her breath, hoping against hope that the past few days and all their revelations might have opened up a new intimacy. She hadn't wanted to admit to being jealous, but obviously he just saw it as sexual jealousy, and not the corrosive emotional kind when you loved someone.

He looked at her and she prayed her eyes weren't giving her away when she felt like crying. She steeled herself.

'I'll come with you to India, of course. I need to meet your family. And attend to business in the hotel.'

Aneesa somehow got out, 'Please don't feel like you should. They'd be perfectly happy to meet you when the baby is born. Believe me, they've gone beyond shock and despair at this stage.'

'Nonetheless, I'll come.'

Aneesa bit her lip so hard she could feel blood. This was it. The line had been drawn. The affair was over. And she knew by going to India now that would be the end. Because he would return to Europe and she wouldn't. Because she would have no reason to.

The following day Sebastian sat in his office. He had any number of things clamouring for his attention, a veritable pile of paperwork that needed to be signed. But he was distracted. Last night, he hadn't slept with Aneesa. She'd been all but monosyllabic on their return from the Grange and had bid him goodnight with definite hands-off signals.

And yet what had he expected? She was going home. He was going to be getting on with his life. It wouldn't be fair to keep sleeping with her, when patently she didn't want it.

He'd just got off the phone to Jacob, who had been telling him some of his plans for Wolfe Manor, and curiously Sebastian felt a measure of peace. Which he'd never expected. It was as if a huge weight had been taken off his shoulders, and his chest. He'd always felt weighed down when he'd thought about his family, especially Jacob, but seeing them at the wedding, he'd realised that they, too, had their preoccupations, their demons. They really weren't as disparate as he'd always imagined.

He thought of the wedding.... It had been such a relief to go upstairs and find Aneesa in his bed...even just knowing that she'd been there—Sebastian stood so quickly in reaction to that unbidden thought his chair went back onto the floor. He heard his assistant ask hesitantly through the phone intercom, 'Is everything all right, Mr Wolfe?'

He smiled grimly. 'Fine, Meredith. Just fine.' He righted the chair and his hand shook slightly.

Everything wasn't just fine. Panic clutched at his gut; everything within him rejected the direction his thoughts had been going in. The last person he'd depended on had been Jacob, and when Jacob had disappeared a fundamental part of Sebastian had been annihilated. And a large part of his trust and faith in mankind had died too.

Depending on anyone was anathema to him and yet somehow Aneesa had infiltrated into that deep secret part of him that he'd vowed would always be invulnerable.

And it still was, he assured himself.

He was losing perspective. He would go to India with Aneesa, meet her family and walk away. She knew the score; at least she and the baby would be provided for.

He told himself that he would be glad, *relieved*, to see the back of her, at least for a while. She'd witnessed him at his most vulnerable too many times for him to even contemplate now. He didn't need that, he'd never asked for that. And he didn't like it. It was why he'd always kept his relationships so impersonal, but from day one Aneesa had come at him like an emotional bulldozer…and just kept coming.

He suddenly felt the urge to go to India that day, and not tomorrow, and had to curb the slightly panicked impulse. He told himself he'd stay at the Mumbai Grand Wolfe Hotel, and limit his time with her family as much as possible. And then get out, and get on with his life.…

Sebastian couldn't be making it any clearer that he was already over their relationship and now it was all about the baby, meeting her family and leaving her in India. Every time she felt like crying Aneesa cursed herself— she'd known exactly what to expect all along, from the moment she'd made the masochistic decision to stay in England.

They were in the first-class cabin of a commercial flight and even though Sebastian was beside her, he might as well have been a million miles away. He'd been brusque to the point of rudeness with her for the past couple of days, had made no attempt to come to her bed and was utterly engrossed in his laptop—as if it held all the secrets to life itself.

Aneesa wondered slightly hysterically if she just opened the emergency door and parachuted out would he even notice. Instead she reclined her seat and pulled a blanket over herself and tried to sleep.

When Aneesa curled up in a ball in her seat facing away from him, Sebastian finally looked over and sighed deeply. Her long black hair was spread out, making him want to run his fingers through its silkiness. The curve of her bottom under the blanket was an enticement to rest his hand there, caressing the tempting line. And her scent was a constant reminder of her innate sensuality which called to him like a homing beacon.

His hands curled into fists as he tried to curb his impulses around her. He put back his head and closed his eyes and wondered if he'd ever feel normal again. He smiled grimly—normal for him anyway. He valiantly blocked out the images that ran through his mind like movie stills of the life he'd always led. He also tried not to remember the way his perfectly unflappable and cool-as-a-cucumber housekeeper, Daniel, had been all but inconsolable saying goodbye to Aneesa, making her own huge brown eyes fill with tears too. Sebastian had felt like an absolute heel, when she was the one that wanted to go home!

He just had to endure a couple of days and then he would make his excuses and go home.

To Aneesa's relief, the press in Mumbai hadn't got wind of her return so their arrival went under the radar. She felt so brittle now that she couldn't have handled the media intrusion along with the prospect of Sebastian leaving in a few days. He hadn't said how long he'd stay but she could well imagine he was already itching to get back.

Mumbai greeted them in all its hot and steamy, chaotic glory. Horns beeping, traffic narrowly avoiding sacred cows and mopeds whizzing by carrying entire families with serene looks on their faces. A beautiful baby with black kohled eyes smiled up at its mother in an auto-rickshaw.

'You really love it here, don't you?' Sebastian asked from the other side of the car. Aneesa nodded. She couldn't look at him, she felt too emotional. So she just said, 'It's home.' But she knew that as much as she loved Mumbai, the minute Sebastian left, it would be flat and empty. Her home was where he was now, and she would never be the same again. In that moment she hated him for doing that to her.

He asked then a little gruffly, 'You should tell me a bit about your family…'

Sudden fire within her made her face him and for the first time she let her guard slip. 'What's the point? I'm sure you've just carved out the minimum time required to meet them to be polite and have made sure you've got plenty of time for business meetings.'

Aneesa flushed. Immediately feeling contrite and terrified that he would guess where her turmoil stemmed from Aneesa said, 'Forget I said that. You didn't deserve that....'

She looked away for a moment and then back, and tried a smile even though it felt forced. Haltingly she started to tell him of her beloved indomitable grandmother who was now apparently clinging onto dear life to see her first grandchild born and had not a word of judgement about Aneesa's less than acceptable status as a single mother.

She told him about her beautiful younger sister who was determined to become a star just like Aneesa albeit without the scandal as she'd declared sunnily to Aneesa on the phone. And about her overweight younger brother who was determined to be a chef, much to their father's chagrin; he just wanted him to love cricket and be a famous cricketer.

By the time her voice faded away she was smiling fondly in earnest, unaware of the tightening in Sebastian's face.

'You love them very much.'

She looked at him and tried not to let the intensity of his blue eyes distract her. 'Yes. I do... But for a long time I took them for granted. I'm lucky that they have loved me so unconditionally.'

Just then she looked past Sebastian out the window and said excitedly, 'We're here!'

Sebastian felt an uncustomary sense of claustrophobia and trepidation crawl over his skin. As the car pulled into a neat driveway he saw a big house emerge, and lined up outside was a veritable welcoming party.

Aneesa jumped out and suddenly a smaller, younger version of herself with a streak of black hair launched herself at Aneesa with a squeal—her younger sister. Her younger brother who was indeed overweight was more nonchalant but one could see that he, too, loved his sister, hugging her with typical teenage awkwardness.

And then her parents… The emotion on their faces nearly made Sebastian want to climb back into the car and drive far, far away. He'd never seen so much naked *love* and affection beaming from anyone. And this was their disgraced daughter?

Aneesa was aware of Sebastian hanging back and she was also aware that he was looking a little green around the gills. She could imagine all too well that this was not a scenario he was used to.

She turned back to him after hugging her parents and took him by the hand. Squeezing it gently, she silently said to him, *Just go with it*, much as he'd done with her when they'd seen his mother. She brought him up to her parents. 'Papa, Mother, I'd like you to meet Sebastian Wolfe.'

CHAPTER NINE

THREE days later, sitting at the dinner table, Sebastian couldn't quite believe that he was still there, amidst the organised chaos of Adani family life. As soon as he'd been pulled into the house, it had been taken for granted that he had to stay. And not only that, but Aneesa's parents had clearly gone out on a limb and challenged their conservative beliefs to put him and Aneesa in a room together.

She'd looked at him miserably once they'd been alone in the bedroom. 'I had no idea they would do this. I'm as shocked as you, believe me. But if I cause a fuss they'll get embarrassed—'

He'd waved a hand. 'It's fine. It's not like we've not shared a room before.'

'No,' Aneesa had said, avoiding his eye. Evidently she hated this as much as he did and just wanted him to return to England so that she could get on with her own life and having the baby.

Something in her demeanour had made his voice sharp. 'Look, I'll stay a couple of days and then I'll have to return anyway, so we can put up with it till then, can't we?'

She'd shrugged insouciantly, making something

even more caustic rise from his belly. 'Sure. I can if you can. I won't have a problem with *this*.' She made a flippant gesture to the king-size bed.

It was in that moment that Sebastian realised how deep was the chasm that had formed between them. It had started the moment she'd announced she wanted to come home. And even though every beat of his pulse cried out to touch her and he ached all over with wanting her, he couldn't touch her.

Now as he looked around the dinner table and took in the affectionate bickering between Akash, Aneesa's brother, and Amrita, her sister, he found that much to his surprise, he felt…comfortable. There was something incredibly soothing about the inconsequential chatter, the fact that they could bicker and tease until Amrita would lean over and pinch Akash's cheek affectionately. His whole life he'd felt on the fringes of things, on the fringes of his own family, and yet here, even though these people were little more than strangers, he felt included in their warmth in a way that stunned him slightly.

Aneesa came out of the kitchen at that moment holding a steaming bowl of vegetables. When she put it down she affectionately ruffled her brother's and sister's heads. They all touched one another all the time… and earlier he'd seen Mr Adani pinch Mrs Adani on her bottom when he'd thought no one was looking.

Sebastian could remember rough-housing with his brothers growing up and his fragile mother's sporadic bursts of being affectionate, but it had never been consistent enough to depend on. He'd certainly never witnessed any kind of affection between his own parents. Their family housekeeper had been motherly but he'd never really felt comfortable when she tried to hug him and he'd get embarrassed when she got emotional after taking him and his brother on their monthly visits to see their mother.

He realised now that he'd always been intensely uncomfortable with any kind of physical intimacy that went beyond the bedroom, and yet with Aneesa, from day one, it had been second nature to touch her, or hold her hand. And he hadn't even noticed.

Watching everything with shrewd black eyes sunk in a wizened face was Aneesa's grandmother, who they all called Beeba. She hadn't said much to Sebastian but she looked at him all the time and he had the uncomfortably prickling sensation that she saw something that he didn't.

As Aneesa came around the table Amrita said, 'Your belly is nearly a proper bump, Neesa. Is the baby kicking yet?'

Mrs Adani chided Amrita and Sebastian felt something fiercely possessive rush through him, almost as if Aneesa's bump was *his*. And yet, it was…but it wasn't, and he felt a wrenching sensation to realise that. And then *he* wanted to know if the baby had started kicking.

Aneesa deflected the attention and sat down beside Sebastian, and her delicate scent wound around him, making his body tighten. He seriously questioned whether he should ask to be put in a separate bedroom that night as the past few nights had been torture. He'd lain awake while Aneesa lay curled up as far away as she could get, and had had to grit his teeth to try and curb his insatiable desires.

Gritting his teeth again, he smiled in answer to

something Amrita had said with a flutter of her long black lashes and tried to block out the welling sensation of something elusively precious slipping out of his grasp.

Aneesa lay in the bed that night and tried to ignore the fact that Sebastian lay just inches away from her. After his initial reaction to her family which had been a bit like a deer stuck in the headlights, he'd somehow relaxed into their unique way of being and interacting. She'd seen him observing everything going on around him, as if fascinated, but not bored, or daunted.

Amrita already had a crush on him. He'd been her audience along with Aneesa when she'd tried out a Bollywood routine she was perfecting for an audition. Her parents were in awe of him, and Beeba, well, she just watched him the same way she watched everyone. And even though Aneesa wasn't in a traditional relationship with him, he'd already been tacitly accepted by her family on a level that Jamal never had been and she could see now how abrasive her ex-fiancé had been within her family.

She knew he was awake next to her and she sighed deeply. There was really no point in pretending anymore.

'Thank you for taking Akash to the hotel to meet with your Michelin-starred chef today. It's possibly the most exciting thing that's ever happened to him. I think you've become his number-one hero for ever.'

Aneesa could feel Sebastian's shrug in the bed beside her.

'It was nothing.'

The silence dragged out but unlike the previous

nights when Aneesa had rolled over and gone to sleep after long torturous minutes, tonight it seemed to be an impossible dream.

Sensation skated over her skin and she was acutely aware of everything. The warm night air swirled around them with the motion of the fan in the ceiling; the scent from the fruit trees outside the window was heavy and luxurious. But worst of all was the mosquito net around the bed which cocooned them in what felt to Aneesa like a sensual prison.

And itching inside her was this awful ravening need to touch Sebastian, to have him touch her. The tension reached screaming point for Aneesa and suddenly terrified that she wouldn't have the strength not to give herself away, she sat up and put on the light.

'Look, I know this is awkward for both of us. You don't want to be here. I'll go to another room. I'll sleep with Amrita.'

She was getting out of the bed when Sebastian snaked out a hand and took her wrist. His touch seared her skin like a brand. 'I thought you didn't want to embarrass your parents. The whole of Mumbai will know by morning if you go to Amrita's room.'

Aneesa tried to yank her wrist away but his grip was too strong. She was crying out inside. 'Well, then, I'll sleep on the floor, or something.'

'Why?' he asked silkily. 'I thought you didn't have a problem with *this*.'

Aneesa all but groaned, kicking herself for having faked such insouciance on that first day. *This* was Sebastian half sitting up, naked from the waist up, his skin burnished gold in the soft light, eyes glittering. Her breasts felt heavy, the peaks tight and tingling painfully. How could she ever not have had a problem with *this*?

Her pride was in tatters as it was. She gritted her teeth and said defiantly, 'So what if I do?'

Inexorably he started to pull her back towards him. 'I never said I didn't want you, Aneesa. I never stopped wanting you.'

She frowned minutely, still resisting his pull. 'But you never tried to…' She trailed off ineffectually, giving herself away spectacularly. Even though she'd struggled to maintain the moral high ground and not give into the excoriating need to have Sebastian make love to her, she'd hungered for him desperately.

'Because I thought you didn't want it, and I thought it was for the best.'

Because they were meant to be going their separate ways.

'But now,' he continued with a glint in his eye that sent a spiral of desire through Aneesa, 'I can see that that reasoning was very flawed. I've been going through torture—wanting you and trying not to touch you.'

Aneesa felt a whole host of conflicting emotions take flight in her chest. On the one hand she wanted to say stop! That he'd been right to do the honourable thing because it would kill her to know the exquisite pleasure of his lovemaking again, but on the other hand…she couldn't imagine going to her death without knowing that pleasure one more time.

Hating herself for her weakness she let him pull her back until she was lying down on her back and he hovered over her. His head dipped but she stopped him with a finger against his lips.

'Wait…when are you going home, Sebastian?' *I need*

to know so I can start to get over you. 'I need to know. I can't...' She stopped. She was so close to showing him how hard it was for her to have him here and see him interacting with her family. 'I just need to get on with things here, my life...'

Something in his face hardened and Aneesa couldn't understand it. Surely he should be looking relieved?

His jaw clenched. 'I have business to attend to at the hotel tomorrow and then I'll be leaving the next day. I'll stay at the hotel tomorrow night.'

Aneesa felt her heart break. 'Good. That's good, then.'

With an almost savage intensity Sebastian slanted his mouth over hers and kissed her. Passion blazed up around them so fierce that Aneesa wondered how the bed didn't catch fire. Her vest top was pulled off. She yanked down her knickers herself, and emitted a gasp of pure pleasure when she felt Sebastian's hot naked body next to hers.

He palmed her breasts, making the peaks tighten into sharp points, and she drew his head down so that he could take a nipple into his mouth. Her belly tightened with pleasure as he suckled her roughly. She met him head-on, biting the skin on his shoulder, and then licking where she'd bitten, revelling in his unique musky taste.

Neither of them could wait, desperation fuelling their movements as Sebastian pushed her legs apart and settled between them. Just before he thrust, with Aneesa's hands on his hips, her legs drawn back, he said with a guttural moan that seemed to be pulled out of him, 'I need this...I need you.'

An ache lodged in her throat and emotion surged as

he thrust deep inside her. And then they were caught up in the familiar dance, which took them higher and higher until every sinew was pulled taut, and when an explosion of intense pleasure gripped her and went on and on, Aneesa wondered how she'd ever be able to cope knowing she'd never have this again.

Long languorous minutes later, sated and lethargic, Aneesa was tucked spoon-like into Sebastian's chest. She could feel him harden again against her bottom and moved sinuously. No matter how tired she might be, she wasn't ready for it to be over yet. Reaching behind to caress his buttocks, she heard a throaty dark chuckle. And then he moved her hair over her shoulder so he could press hot kisses onto the back of her neck.

With a powerful move of his hips, he found where she still ached for him and thrust up, his arms a tight bind around her, one hand on her breast. Her head fell back, and as he thrust again and again until she couldn't breathe or think, he kissed her so sweetly that she couldn't stop the tears falling.

When the storm was over, Aneesa was replete and exhausted. Awash with emotion. She took his hand from where it was wrapped around her, entwined in hers, and pressed a kiss to it. And just before she let exhaustion take her away, she thought of the words that had been trembling on her lips for days now. 'I love you.'

Sebastian stilled. Had she just said— His mind blanked. Her breaths were already deep and even. Perhaps he'd imagined it? He couldn't process the information straight away, not when he couldn't think because his brain was mush after two of the most powerful orgasms he could ever remember having.

One hand rested on Aneesa's rounded belly and just as his head was beginning to whirl at the implication of her words, *if* she'd even said them, he felt the tiniest most subtle of sensations against his fingers. A mere flutter, like a small heartbeat. Holding his breath, he spread his hand out and it came again, against the palm of his hand this time. Tiny, barely noticeable. But there. His baby.

He lay awake like that for a long time. Until the rising sun started to streak the sky outside with the most delicate pink trails.

And then he quietly slipped out of the bed and left.

CHAPTER TEN

ANEESA woke the next morning, her body feeling deliciously weighted down in the bed. She smiled and stretched and it was only then that she realised that she was naked and the previous night came back to her. Her eyes flew open.

She was alone in the bed and from the feel of where Sebastian would have lain, it was cold and had been for some time. They'd made love, and he'd left. A wrenching pain made Aneesa gasp and pull her legs up so that she curled in a foetal position. This was it. He was gone.

For a couple of minutes she felt so cold that she wondered if she might be sick. Which was crazy when it would be nearly thirty degrees outside.

Only when she was afraid her mother would come to see where she was did she get out of bed. But when she approached the kitchen and dining area she nearly stumbled. Amrita was exclaiming petulantly, 'I can't believe he would go without saying goodbye to *me*!'

Aneesa had to sit on the bottom step of the stairs. Her skin had gone clammy. Until that moment she hadn't known for sure that he had gone. She heard her mother's placating voice and heard footsteps.

'Aneesa, are you OK?'

It was Akash. She smiled and stood, feeling her blood rush southwards, and suddenly everything was swirling and blackness enfolded her.

She woke to a sea of concerned faces and struggled to sit up, finding that she was on the couch in the sitting room. She was pushed back down firmly.

'You, young lady, are not moving. The doctor is on his way.'

She protested but was drowned out. She wanted to cry out that she'd just fainted—she didn't need anyone or anything. *Just Sebastian and his undying love.* That ridiculously futile thought made her smile slightly and her mother smiled too, with relief, obviously misinter-preting it.

She fussed around Aneesa. 'You need to be careful, Neesa, you're taking after me. I fainted all the time when I was pregnant....'

The rest of the family slipped away and Aneesa asked her mother casually, 'Did you see Sebastian before he left today?'

Her mother shook her head and then said, 'I think he left something for you—a note. Let me get it.'

In the space of time it took for her mother to come back, Aneesa was nearly climbing the walls. She all but grabbed the note and when her mother wasn't moving she said, 'I think I need to rest for a bit...I'll be fine.'

With a kiss to her forehead, making her feel as if she was a teenager all over again, her mother left. Taking a deep breath, Aneesa opened the note and read the confident scrawl: *Can you meet me at my suite this evening—7:00 p.m.? Sebastian.*

Aneesa crumpled the note into her fist. She refused

to acknowledge the treacherous flutters in her belly. It would only be because he wanted to sort out arrangements for coming back to see the baby or something like that.

The doctor came soon afterwards and declared that everything was fine and that Aneesa just needed to eat. So she was waited upon and force-fed for the entire day by her well-meaning family. But nothing could stop the sensation of cold sneaking into her bloodstream as if some life force was being cut off.

That evening, like an automaton, she got dressed to go to the hotel in a long stretchy black jersey dress. For the first time she'd noticed that she couldn't get into her jeans anymore. She put make-up on her eyes purely to disguise the shadows underneath and to feel like she had some armour on. Slipping into flat sandals and draping a long shawl around her shoulders that she could pull over her head and belly to disguise herself, sari-style, she left the house for the hotel.

Despite her disguise, the minute she walked into the foyer of the luxurious hotel, a man stepped forward and said obsequiously, 'Miss Adani?'

She nodded. And he gestured with a hand. 'Please, allow me to show you to Mr Wolfe's suite.'

Of course, she realised a little hysterically. It wasn't as if she'd ever gone to or come from his suite by the conventional route the first time around.

They ascended in a lift marked *Private* and came to a smooth halt all too soon. Aneesa's palms felt sweaty and her heart was beating unevenly. She prayed she wouldn't faint again.

The concierge, or manager, ushered her out and

opened the door to the suite. 'Have a good evening, Miss Adani.'

And then the door was shut behind her. Aneesa let the shawl drop from her head to her shoulders. Déjà vu washed over her with bittersweet nostalgia. The suite was much the same as it had been that night. It appeared to be empty, only one or two lamps throwing out little halos of golden light.

She could see though that there were lights coming from the terrace, and the sliding doors were open, sending the evening breeze drifting through. The evening was a dusky opalescent colour outside and Aneesa could see the ubiquitous Indian kites floating against the darkening sky as people practiced off their rooftops.

A sudden feeling of anger gripped her. Why wasn't Sebastian meeting her downstairs in more anonymous surroundings, under brighter lights? She hated him for bringing her back into this seductive world. And where was he anyway? Aneesa suddenly needed air, needed to breathe before she saw Sebastian and faced the final demise of their relationship as lovers, before it became about the logistics of parenting from their respective countries and homes.

She made for the terrace and assumed he was in the office room, perhaps catching up on a call. She walked straight outside and went to the ornately carved stone wall. Gripping it, she took a deep breath, much as she had that night all those weeks before.

And, exactly like that night, a voice from behind her drawled seductively, 'Please don't tell me you're thinking of jumping.'

Aneesa's heart stopped, and started again with

an uneven beat. This time she didn't whirl around in shock and surprise. She stayed where she was for a long moment, and then steeled herself before turning to face Sebastian, and when she did she nearly fell down all over again. He was devastatingly handsome, even dressed in just a white shirt and dark trousers. But it was as if she was seeing him for the first time.

She smiled bitterly in reaction. 'I had no intention of jumping that night, and I certainly have no intention of jumping now. No man is worth that.'

He strolled towards her then with hands in his pockets, making her want to take in his lean hips. She fought the urge to look.

'But what you're implying with that statement is that you've weighed up the possibility and found it lacking…'

Aneesa snorted and felt a little bewildered. Why was Sebastian being so…seductive? Why wasn't he being all businesslike? Something caught her eye behind him…*and why was there a table for two set for dinner complete with a softly flickering candle and an ice bucket with champagne?*

Pain gripped her so hard she saw stars. She garbled out, 'Oh, God…I'm sorry. You have a date. You were out here preparing and I came out…'

She went to walk back inside but suddenly Sebastian was there, gripping her arm. Her shawl fell to the ground.

'No, no one else is coming here, Aneesa, it's just you and me.'

'But…' Her voice wouldn't work. She swallowed. 'Why? Like this? I thought you just wanted to discuss arrangements.'

He dropped her arm from his grip and for the first time she saw a crack in his composure. He ran a hand through his hair. 'I guess I do…in a way.'

Aneesa felt seriously overwhelmed and was afraid that, much like last night, she'd end up doing or saying something to give herself away spectacularly.

Sebastian looked at her so intensely though that she couldn't think straight.

'Do you remember after we made love last night… do you remember saying anything?'

Aneesa forced her sluggish brain to work. What on earth could he be—? She froze. Every part of her body froze. She remembered now, in chilling detail. She'd whispered the fateful words. She'd thought she'd just said them in her head. But she'd said them *out loud*. No wonder he'd left so fast this morning.

She tried to back away but couldn't because the wall was behind her. She alternately shook and nodded her head, her brain imploding. 'I…I'm not sure what you mean…'

Sebastian was grim. 'You said you loved me.'

Any hope of retaining dignity fled in an instant. Aneesa gulped. 'Well…I may have…I mean, I don't remember but perhaps afterwards…but it didn't mean anything.'

A muscle in his jaw twitched. 'So it was just a help-less transitory emotional response to a physical act? Is that what you're saying?'

Aneesa gulped again. Sebastian looked so formi-dable. And then she seemed to regain some sanity, or at least equilibrium. 'Why, Sebastian? Why do you even care what I might have said? You've made it very clear all along that nothing would come of this relationship except two adults having a baby. From the moment I arrived in England you fought my presence.

'So what on earth does it matter to you what I might have said, or what I might feel? You're leaving tomorrow.'

'Am I?' He laughed but it sounded pained. 'To be honest, I don't know if I'm coming or going and I've been feeling like that for a long time now....'

He brushed past her then to rest his hands on the stone balustrade, and dropped his head between his shoulders. Something about him looked so tortured in that moment that Aneesa had to fight back the urge to put out her hand to touch him in comfort.

His head came up and his eyes speared hers. 'But I've also been feeling alive, and *connected*, for the first time in my life.'

He stood tall again and Aneesa felt curiously weightless. He reached out a hand and curled it around her jaw, fingers around her neck under the heavy fall of her hair. She could feel a slight tremor in his hand and her heart tripped.

'I never...wanted to create a family. I never wanted to marry. I never wanted to fall in love. I had no frame of reference for all of those things that most people aspire to, and take for granted. I've always been terrified that something of my father's twisted genes was lying dormant in me and that basic happiness was something I could never have, as if I was jinxed in some way.

'But seeing Nathaniel get married, and Jacob come home to try and make amends...seeing him come to terms with the past, and the way he's trying to bring us together again, has changed my perspective. Hearing you say you love me last night—whether you meant it or not, it freed something inside me. I hadn't allowed myself to think that you could possibly have feelings for me. You'd only come to me because of the baby...

'These past few days, being with your family... It's so...easy. They're easy. Love for them is freely given and taken. You have no idea what it's like to witness that, to experience it as a reality, not just an elusive concept.' He smiled bleakly. 'Well, you do. You've grown up with it. It's why you're so open and so...honest.'

Aneesa felt like cringing amidst the shock at what he was saying. He had to be referring to her constant nagging and questioning to get him to open up and spill his innermost secrets.

He seemed to struggle with something, his hand still on her jaw, and finally said, 'My family...you've seen something of what we experienced. It's not an excuse but perhaps it's how I can explain to you why it's taken me so long to realise the most important thing of my life.'

Sebastian put his other hand on her jaw now and stepped in close. Inexplicably tears started to fill Aneesa's eyes and she wasn't even sure why she was crying. Sebastian smiled. 'Your eyes...do you know that they are like two worlds of emotion? The first night we met I was in awe of how expressive they were.'

Aneesa struggled for control, but couldn't speak.

'Last night, I felt our baby move...'

Aneesa frowned. She'd felt flutters for a few days now but had put it down to Sebastian's effect on her.

'...and for the first time I really felt connected to him...or her. This baby is mine, *ours*. And I don't want it to be brought up on two different continents, being shuttled back and forth on holidays. Isolated. A lonely child.'

Aneesa sobered up, her tears cleared. She had a feeling she knew exactly what Sebastian was getting at now, what he meant by 'the most important thing.' He wanted to do the right thing, take care of them, because now he felt he could deal with it. And because she'd stupidly revealed that she had feelings for him. She took down his hands.

'Sebastian, I know you've been through a lot with your family and I'm so sorry that you had to go through that. But believe me, with the greatest will in the world, a relationship that's not based on love is not going to be the best thing for your child. Our child. I'm sorry if that sounds impossibly idealistic to you and I can see that you've had some revelations, but please…don't make us do this.'

She looked away because those damn tears were coming back. She felt rather than heard a movement and looked down when she felt her hand being tugged into Sebastian's. He was on one knee at her feet and the tears sprang in earnest.

She shook her head. 'Please, Sebastian, don't…you don't know how cruel it is.'

He looked up at her. 'What would be cruel is if you were to turn your back on me and deny me the only chance of happiness I'll ever have.'

He gripped her hand tighter. 'You may or may not have meant what you said last night, but all day I've been praying that you did. Aneesa…I'm in love with you. I'm so fathoms-deep in love with you that I'm drowning. I've been falling for you since the moment our eyes met that evening, when you looked at me and made my world go spinning in the other direction. But I had no idea what was happening. Not until we came back here…and I saw what love is, and recognised it for the first time in my life.

'It's as if I've had emotional dyslexia—every time you got a bit closer, I pushed you away because it threatened every bit of self-defence I'd built up over the years.'

He took something out of his pocket and Aneesa saw a ring, a simple princess-cut diamond, about half the size of her first engagement ring and already infinitely more precious. Her throat was clogged with emotion and shock and the incredible burgeoning hope that perhaps this was real.

'I can't live without you, Aneesa.' His eyes were intense. 'I would die. It's that simple. And the thought of having this baby still terrifies me but I know that if you're by my side, I might just have a chance of not ruining my child's existence completely.

'So please—' with a shaking hand he put the ring on her finger '—will you wear this ring…and be my lover and my best friend, for ever. I want to marry you but I know how you feel about the prospect of going through that again and I wouldn't do that to you unless you wanted it….'

Aneesa tugged Sebastian up until he stood before her. She finally managed to get out through the rising emotion, 'I did mean it…last night. I couldn't hold it in. I'd been holding it in for so long that I knew it would come out eventually. That's why I wanted to come home. I thought you'd end up hating me for intruding into your life so much. I came to you because I was pregnant, yes, but I hadn't stopped thinking about you since that night. I would have wanted to see you again no matter what....'

Sebastian took her face in his hands and kissed her so passionately that she felt dizzy and then he picked her up and carried her into the bedroom where they'd made love that first night. Where their baby had been conceived.

With tenderness infusing every moment, they made love again. And afterwards, wrapped in the circle of Sebastian's arms, Aneesa said softly, 'I feel like this is a dream. I'm afraid I'll wake up and you'll be gone.'

He pulled her right into him and put his hand over hers on her belly, over their baby, and said huskily with humour lacing his voice, 'If *I* can believe, then you definitely can. And the baby agrees, can you feel him?'

Aneesa held her breath and there it was, the tiniest of flutters against their joined hands. They seemed to be growing stronger by the minute, along with her belief that this *was* real, and that with the indestructible force of love between them, anything would be possible, even a second attempt at marriage.

As if Sebastian could hear her thoughts, he spoke close to her ear. 'We could go to my island, and get married on the beach. With just my staff as witnesses...'

Incredible joy bubbled up inside Aneesa and she turned so that she could look up into Sebastian's face. It was completely open, no shadows or secrets lurking in those blue eyes anymore, and her heart turned over.

She smiled. 'I'd like that.'

Sebastian frowned for a second. 'Would your parents mind?'

Aneesa smiled ruefully. 'I think they would be forever grateful not to have to go through anything approximating a public wedding again.'

Sebastian grinned and kissed her with achingly slow sweetness and then drew back. With a mischievous glint in his eye he said carefully, 'You remember when you said you regretted the fact that you hadn't asked your aunts and cousins to do your henna tattoo ritual when you had the chance?'

She nodded, feeling a flame start to ignite in her belly.

'Well, if you wanted to give them the chance to do it over again, I wouldn't mind....'

Aneesa looked mock shocked. 'Sebastian Wolfe, are you telling me that you have developed a wedding henna tattoo fetish?'

He came over her then and she exulted in his solid weight between her legs which she was already opening to entice him to a more intimate position. Between kisses, he growled, 'I have an Aneesa Adani fetish. Just be thankful that I got the whole unwrapping-the-Indian-princess-on-her-wedding-night out of my system. Otherwise I'd have you laden down with jewels and in a sari all over again. As it is I'm willing to settle for a simple white dress, no shoes, our baby bump and the tattoo....'

Aneesa twined her arms around Sebastian's neck and arched into him. 'Do you know,' she said a little unsteadily, because she felt emotional at the thought of 'our baby bump' and also because Sebastian's hand was exploring between her legs, 'that when I have the tattoo done they'll write your name within the design and you won't be allowed to sleep with me till you find it....'

'Well, then, tell them to make it small and hard to

find because I'm going to enjoy making you beg for mercy and curse their artistic ingenuity.'

Aneesa gasped her pleasure out loud when he joined their bodies. And for the next few minutes, she was happy to forget about anything but this blissful moment which held within it the promise of all their blissful moments to come.

* * * * *

Harlequin *Presents*

Coming Next Month

from **Harlequin Presents® EXTRA**. Available September 13, 2011.

Coming Next Month

from **Harlequin Presents®**. Available September 27, 2011.

Visit www.HarlequinInsideRomance.com
for more information on upcoming titles!

REQUEST YOUR FREE BOOKS!

Harlequin *Presents*

2 FREE NOVELS PLUS
2 FREE GIFTS!

PASSION GUARANTEED SEDUCTION

YES! Please send me 2 FREE Harlequin Presents® novels and my 2 FREE gifts (gifts are worth about $10). After receiving them, if I don't wish to receive any more books, I can return the shipping statement marked "cancel." If I don't cancel, I will receive 6 brand-new novels every month and be billed just $4.30 per book in the U.S. or $4.99 per book in Canada. That's a saving of at least 14% off the cover price! It's quite a bargain! Shipping and handling is just 50¢ per book in the U.S. and 75¢ per book in Canada.* I understand that accepting the 2 free books and gifts places me under no obligation to buy anything. I can always return a shipment and cancel at any time. Even if I never buy another book, the two free books and gifts are mine to keep forever.

106/306 HDN FERQ

Name _____ (PLEASE PRINT) _____

Address _____ Apt. # _____

City _____ State/Prov. _____ Zip/Postal Code _____

Signature (if under 18, a parent or guardian must sign)

Mail to the Reader Service:
IN U.S.A.: P.O. Box 1867, Buffalo, NY 14240-1867
IN CANADA: P.O. Box 609, Fort Erie, Ontario L2A 5X3

Not valid for current subscribers to Harlequin Presents books.

**Are you a current subscriber to Harlequin Presents books
and want to receive the larger-print edition?
Call 1-800-873-8635 or visit www.ReaderService.com.**

* Terms and prices subject to change without notice. Prices do not include applicable taxes. Sales tax applicable in N.Y. Canadian residents will be charged applicable taxes. Offer not valid in Quebec. This offer is limited to one order per household. All orders subject to credit approval. Credit or debit balances in a customer's account(s) may be offset by any other outstanding balance owed by or to the customer. Please allow 4 to 6 weeks for delivery. Offer available while quantities last.

Your Privacy—The Reader Service is committed to protecting your privacy. Our Privacy Policy is available online at www.ReaderService.com or upon request from the Reader Service.

We make a portion of our mailing list available to reputable third parties that offer products we believe may interest you. If you prefer that we not exchange your name with third parties, or if you wish to clarify or modify your communication preferences, please visit us at www.ReaderService.com/consumerchoice or write to us at Reader Service Preference Service, P.O. Box 9062, Buffalo, NY 14269. Include your complete name and address.

HP11B

*Harlequin Romantic Suspense presents the latest book
in the scorching new* KELLEY LEGACY *miniseries
from best-loved veteran series author Carla Cassidy*

*Scandal is the name of the game as the Kelley family fights
to preserve their legacy, their hearts...and their lives.*

*Read on for an excerpt from the fourth title
RANCHER UNDER COVER*

*Available October 2011
from Harlequin Romantic Suspense*

"**W**ould you like a drink?" Caitlin asked as she walked
to the minibar in the corner of the room. She felt as if she
needed to chug a beer or two for courage.

"No, thanks. I'm not much of a drinking man," he
replied.

She raised an eyebrow and looked at him curiously as she
poured herself a glass of wine. "A ranch hand who doesn't
enjoy a drink? I think maybe that's a first."

He smiled easily. "There was a six-month period in my
life when I drank too much. I pulled myself out of the bottom of a bottle a little over seven years ago and I've never
looked back."

"That's admirable, to know you have a problem and then
fix it."

Those broad shoulders of his moved up and down in
an easy shrug. "I don't know how admirable it was, all I
knew at the time was that I had a choice to make between
living and dying and I decided living was definitely more
appealing."

She wanted to ask him what had happened preceding
that six-month period that had plunged him into the bottom

of the bottle, but she didn't want to know too much about him. Personal information might produce a false sense of intimacy that she didn't need, didn't want in her life.

"Please, sit down," she said, and gestured him to the table. She had never felt so on edge, so awkward in her life.

"After you," he replied.

She was aware of his gaze intensely focused on her as she rounded the table and sat in the chair, and she wanted to tell him to stop looking at her as if she were a delectable dessert he intended to savor later.

Watch Caitlin and Rhett's sensual saga unfold amidst the shocking, ripped-from-the-headlines drama of the Kelley Legacy miniseries in

RANCHER UNDER COVER

Available October 2011 only from Harlequin Romantic Suspense, wherever books are sold.

USA TODAY bestselling author

Carol Marinelli

brings you her new romance

HEART OF THE DESERT

One searing kiss is all it takes for Georgie to know
Sheikh Prince Ibrahim is trouble....

But, trapped in the swirling sands, Georgie finally
surrenders to the brooding rebel prince—yet the
law of his land decrees that she can never
really be his....

Available October 2011.

Available only from Harlequin Presents®.

SPECIAL EDITION

Life, Love and Family

Look for
NEW YORK TIMES AND *USA TODAY*
BESTSELLING AUTHOR

KATHLEEN EAGLE

in October!

Recently released and wounded war vet
Cal Cougar is determined to start his recovery—
inside and out. There's no better place than the
Double D Ranch to begin the journey.
Cal discovers firsthand how extraordinary the
ranch really is when he meets a struggling single
mom and her very special child.

ONE BRAVE COWBOY,
available September 27 wherever books are sold!